The Indian showed himself and then stepped out into plain sight. Slocum drew a bead on him but held his fire. He was playing for bigger stakes. Two more Indians showed themselves. Another, and then the rest, all standing in a tight knot to discuss what was going on.

Slocum opened fire, levering in new rounds as fast as he could pull back on the trigger. The rifle barrel turned red-hot from the passage of so much lead so fast . . .

JAKE LOGAN

SLOCUM AND THE POMO CHIEF

JOVE BOOKS, NEW YORK

SLOCUM AND THE POMO CHIEF

A Jove Book / published by arrangement with the author

PRINTING HISTORY
Jove edition / June 2000

All rights reserved.
Copyright © 2000 by Penguin Putnam Inc.
This book may not be reproduced in whole or in part, by mimeograph or any other means, without permission.
For information address: The Berkley Publishing Group, a division of Penguin Putnam Inc., 375 Hudson Street, New York, New York 10014.

The Penguin Putnam Inc. World Wide Web site address is http://www.penguinputnam.com

ISBN: 0-515-12838-4

A JOVE BOOK®
Jove Books are published by The Berkley Publishing Group, a division of Penguin Putnam Inc., 375 Hudson Street, New York, New York 10014. JOVE and the "J" design are trademarks belonging to Penguin Putnam Inc.

PRINTED IN THE UNITED STATES OF AMERICA

10 9 8 7 6 5 4 3 2 1

1

John Slocum stared at the stack of grimy white and faded red poker chips on the table in front of him and sucked in his breath. He had less than half the stake he'd started with an hour ago. Carefully fanning his cards, he studied the full house, deuces over queens.

"So what's it gonna be?" growled the bulky sailor seated on the far side of the beer-stained wooden table. The man sneered and his eyes were brighter than the day-time sun. The bright pink knife scar starting at the corner of his mouth puckered as he tried to smile and take some of the edge off his demand for Slocum to pony up still more money.

You caught more flies with honey than vinegar, and Slocum's money was like honey to this bear of a sailor.

The pot held damned near two hundred dollars. Slocum needed the money, but the other player's sudden change in attitude warned him. A full house was hard to beat—but it could be beaten. Considering the run of lousy luck he had experienced in the past few months since he had drifted into San Francisco from down south along the Monterey coast, he was worried that the sailor held the best in the deck, and worrying wasn't something Slocum ought to do while he played. There was an ebb and flow in any game he had to ride with, just as the sailor rode the tides. And like the experienced sea captain, Slocum had learned not to oppose the flow.

The hand was good. But it didn't feel right. He ran the risk of bucking the feelings that had kept him alive ever since the war. But the money . . .

"So?" the sailor said gruffly, leaning forward. Meaty hands pressed flat on the table as if he intended to lever himself to a full standing position. Slocum had watched the man when he came into the Cobweb Palace Saloon at the end of a pier on the Embarcadero. He was taller than Slocum's six-foot height by more than three inches. Slocum weighed close to two hundred. The sailor weighed a hundred pounds more—and not much of it was fat. He moved easily, quickly, powerfully, with the look of a man itching for a fight. Any hint of drunkenness was only a guise. His eyes told exactly how sober, and eager, he was.

"What the hell," Slocum said, pushing the remainder of his chips into the center of the table. "I'll call."

Slocum did not have to see the other man's hand to know he had lost. But the straight flush, king high, mocked him as the cards caught the dim light from gas lamps spaced randomly around inside the cobweb-decorated saloon.

"You beat that?" demanded the sailor.

Slocum dropped his cards onto the table, worrying about something and not knowing what it was. He had the feeling he had been cheated, but how?

His eyes narrowed as he reached across and pushed the cards dropped by the sailor apart on the table so each lay separate from the others.

"Get yer hands away from those cards," the sailor said. The growl from deep in his chest didn't have an accompanying attempt at smiling this time.

"The queen of diamonds," Slocum said.

"What about 'er?"

Slocum turned his hand over and showed the others at the table. One of the pair of queens he held was a queen of diamonds.

"Funny-looking deck to have two of the same card, isn't it?"

"You sayin' somethin', matey?" The sailor rose to his full height. He cracked his knuckles as he tightened his hands into fists the size of quart jars.

Slocum stood and stepped away from the table, hands easy at his side. His Colt Navy hung in a cross-draw holster at his left side, but even a drunk could tell he was ready to draw if the sailor took so much as a single step forward.

"You cheated me. Maybe not you, but one of them," Slocum said, casting his steely green gaze around the table. He figured two of the men, the ones looking frightened and perplexed, had had nothing to do with the cheating. The other two were shifting weight in their chairs, reaching for concealed weapons of their own. Those two and the sailor were in cahoots.

"Two of them," Slocum amended, turning slightly so he could draw and get shots off at both of the men still in their chairs.

"What's goin' on?" roared a bouncer, pushing his way through the crowd already forming a ring around the table. Side bets were being made on who would walk away if shooting started. Slocum overheard enough to know he was racking up heavy odds against him. That told him even more. The men who had so cleverly cheated him were well known in the Cobweb Palace Saloon.

He and good luck had been strangers too long. Slocum knew he would be floating facedown in San Francisco Bay in a heartbeat if he pressed the matter.

"Nothing," Slocum said, stepping back but keeping the three in view. The sailor laughed raucously, then called for drinks for the entire house. This produced a rush to the bar. Slocum swallowed his bile. The rabble in the saloon were drinking on *his* money.

He stepped outside onto the docks and was surprised to find the sun poking up over the bay to the east. The poker game—the fleecing—had taken most of the night. Slocum considered ways of getting his money back, then shook his head in disgust. They had cheated him, and they had done it expertly. Except for the blunder in the last hand, he would never have known.

"Learn from it," Slocum said, walking briskly down the dock and turning toward Portsmouth Square. He had no idea where he was headed. His horse had pulled up lame, and he'd sold the mare for ten dollars after arriving in San Francisco. Some worn gear stashed at the livery was all he owned.

He enjoyed being footloose and fancy-free, but this was ridiculous.

A man on the far side of the square caught his attention. Standing on a box, the man wasn't selling. He was recruiting.

"Carpenters," the man shouted. "Good wages, pay at the end of every day. Need experienced carpenters right away."

"How much?" asked Slocum, going to stand beside him. The man glanced down and dismissed him right away.

"We don't need gunmen. We need carpenters."

"I've been swinging a hammer down south. I know my way around a saw and rule," Slocum said.

"Where?"

"A lady down San Jose way keeps carpenters working

around the clock. I spent a week or so working for her."

"Who was foreman?" the man demanded.

"A man by the name of John Hansen. Had a wife and two boys."

" 'Nuff said," the man replied, changing his tone. "If you worked at the Winchester house you're right for this job."

"You don't want to know why I left?"

The man chuckled. "Nobody—except Hansen—stays long there. Hell, I spent danged near a month workin' for the crazy lady myself. Git on over there and jump into the back of my wagon and you can start right away."

"Suits me," Slocum said. He climbed into the rear of the cargo wagon, already laden with a dozen kegs of nails, and waited another half hour while the man pitched the delectations of carpentry to passersby in the square. The three men joining Slocum had less the look of carpenters than vagabonds. But the recruiter had promised five dollars a day, princely wages Slocum wasn't going to turn down.

"Hang on tight," the man said, climbing into the driver's box. The wagon creaked and groaned and began to move as the mules strained to pull their load up a steep hill. Slocum was familiar enough with San Francisco to know they were headed for the Russian Hill section, an area filled with swank houses where the town's rich preferred to live.

"Get to it," the man said. "We got a house to build!"

Slocum dropped his six-shooter on top of his shirt and set to work, sweating soon enough in spite of the damp wetness of the San Francisco day. By noon he was running short of wood. He brushed off his hands and went to the man who had recruited him. The man had a worried look Slocum did not like.

"Need more studs to finish off that back room," Slocum said.

"We need more of everything," the foreman said with a sigh. "Reckon I'm gonna have to let the lot of you go."

"What?" came the angry cry from the half-dozen men who had gathered when Slocum made his request for more lumber.

"There's a building boom in Frisco," the foreman said. "I could work you all ten hours a day every day of the week and never come close to meeting quotas. But there's no more lumber. Every other job in town's eating it all up."

"You gonna pay us?" demanded one of the other carpenters. Slocum picked up his shirt and wiped his face with it. The foreman saw how Slocum also kept his hand near the six-gun. Licking his lips, the foreman nodded.

"A full day's pay. You've all earned it, and it ain't your fault I can't get more sawed lumber. I been tryin', I have."

As the man paid out the full day's wages for a mere three hours' work, Slocum tucked his salary into his shirt pocket and asked, "Where's the lumber come from?"

"North," the man said. "Up Fort Bragg way. Brand-new company starting to cut redwoods there, but the demand's bigger 'n any supply, even movin' the lumber on a railroad."

Slocum nodded, then turned and looked across the Golden Gate. North was as good a direction as any. If San Francisco needed lumber and it was being sawed up north, logging had to be a steadier job than swinging a claw hammer, then waiting for more planks to be cut and delivered.

It took Slocum four hours and fifty cents to get across the Bay on the ferry, and another two hours before he found the railroad mentioned by the foreman back on Russian Hill. He had enough money to keep him going a few days, thanks to the all-too-brief stint at carpentry, but Slocum smelled bigger money and steadier work. He was no stranger to long, backbreaking hours. He had ridden herd on many a cattle roundup. The best thing about those months on the dreary, dusty trails had been steady grub and the promise of a few dollars at the end of the drive.

Right now, he'd settle for the steady grub.

"What you nosin' around for?" demanded a dapper man incongruously wearing a fancy bowler and a lumberjack's plaid shirt and canvas pants that looked to be starched.

Slocum settled down on a hitching rail and pointed toward the train depot across the street of the small town that didn't seem to have much in the way of a name.

"Worked down in San Francisco until they ran out of lumber. Figured it was a good move to see if supplying the lumber was any better than building houses with it."

"You don't look much like a carpenter," the man said, squinting at Slocum. He took in the low-slung six-shooter and the set to Slocum's shoulders. "You got it in you to work as a lumberjack?"

"Never done it, but I'm a fast learner."

"Long hours, grueling work. Dangerous too."

"Danger and I are old friends. We got an accommodation," Slocum said. "It passes me by, and I don't call out to it."

The man laughed and shoved out his hand. "My name's Spence, and I'm the foreman of the Fort Bragg Lumber Company owned by C. R. Johnson. We're in desperate need of men willing to work for their pay."

"As lumberjacks?"

"If I filled that whole damn train, it wouldn't be

enough," Spence said, pointing to the engine chugging into the station. "I've been recruitin', but help's mighty scarce these days."

"Boom times," Slocum agreed. "Don't help much that gold's still being found all over Northern California."

"Why'd you say that?" Spence snapped.

"Because it's true. I hear the rumors. Back in '49 was only the start."

"Those fools went bankrupt and beggin'. The real fortune's to be made supplying things for building. Sutter went bust when he could have made a fortune," Spence said, still somewhat belligerently. Slocum figured Spence had gone out to the goldfields himself and come up with a worthless claim. That'd explain his attitude.

"I'm no prospector," Slocum said. "I want to eat three squares and get some money for a poke."

"Then you're the man C. R. wants," Spence said. "Climb on into the passenger car. We'll be makin' the trip back to Fort Bragg within the hour. You got any gear?"

Slocum shook his head. What little he had was still in the San Francisco livery and was likely to remain there a good long time. The saddle was nothing special, and the saddlebags held nothing but memories of more prosperous days.

"A man who travels light," Spence said, almost in admiration. "You kin git more clothes from the company store 'fore we git out into the woods." With that, the foreman took off to round up a half-dozen other men, all of whom looked to be experienced lumberjacks from the way they walked and acted.

Slocum climbed into the passenger car and sank to a seat, leaning back and tipping his hat down over his eyes. He thought to catch a few winks before the train left the station, but a puppy-dog-eager youth who couldn't have been older than eighteen bounced into the train and flopped bonelessly into the seat across the aisle from Slocum.

"You goin' up north too? To saw them redwoods down?"

"Reckon so," Slocum allowed. He wasn't feeling overly sociable, but he saw what he wanted wasn't going to matter to this young man.

"Never been up there before. You?" He did not wait for Slocum to shake his head before rambling on. "Fort Bragg's named after a Reb general."

"Braxton Bragg," Slocum said.

"You know?" The youth sagged a little, his thunder stolen away. "Think it rare as horse feathers to name a town after a Reb general."

"Braxton Bragg was a good man," Slocum said. He had never served under him, but knew many who had. Most all of them had praised Bragg, certainly more than others like the hidebound John Bell Hood or the flamboyant, utterly reckless Nathan Bedford Forrest.

"You a Johnny Reb?"

"I'm an American," Slocum said, and then introduced himself. He had no desire to rehash the war with this brash young upstart. The war carried too many painful memories, from his brother Robert's death to the way his family farm had been seized by a carpetbagger judge for unpaid taxes. That judge had come to confiscate the farm from Slocum and had ended up dead and buried.

And on balance, Slocum considered those good memories. Riding with Quantrill and his butchers and being shot in the belly by Bloody Bill Anderson for complaining about slaughtering eight-year-olds were more nightmares than memories for him.

"Billy Buggs," the youth said. "My friends call me Billy."

"Fancy that," Slocum said.

"Yep, I'm goin' up to saw down the redwoods. My pa thinks it'll be a good profession since our store in San Francisco's not been doin' so good. Besides, I'm the youngest and my older brother's goin' to inherit the store. Who wants to work for Peter?"

"Not me," Slocum said, trying to ignore the way Billy Buggs ran off at the mouth. Spence came through with a dozen men, who sank into seats scattered throughout the car. Then the engine began huffing and puffing as it started north.

Slocum thought it would give him a chance to rest up, but something about the way Spence seemed keyed up kept Slocum from drifting off to sleep. Even Billy Buggs settled down to a relative quiet, but Spence kept fingering a Smith & Wesson .44 Russian tucked into his belt, as if he expected trouble.

When the bullets started flying an hour after they left the station, breaking glass in the car windows, Slocum was ready for it.

2

Slocum glanced around the car at the other men as the train screeched to a halt. Many dived for cover under the seats. None had the look of a gent willing to fight for himself. And most of them looked seedier than the carpenters being recruited back in San Francisco for day work. Slocum reckoned Spence needed men so bad he didn't care what they looked like or what their experience might be.

He just wished the foreman had picked a few men with backbones.

Slocum whipped out his six-shooter and used the barrel to knock out the glass that hadn't been shot away in the window.

"What's goin' on?" Billy Buggs asked breathlessly.

"Keep your damn fool head down," Slocum snapped. "Unless you want it shot off." Even as he issued the warning, another fusillade ripped through the car. Slocum counted, waited for a second round of fire, then chanced a quick look outside the train after the bullets had ripped away even more wood and glass.

Two Indians decked out in gaudy war paint whooped and hollered and fired their rifles frantically. Slocum coolly leveled his Colt Navy and squeezed off a round.

The range was extreme for a six-shooter, but he was a better shot with the pistol than the Indians with their rifles. One Indian yelped and clawed at his arm where Slocum's slug cut a bloody groove. Then the pair of attacking Indians were left behind as the engineer got the train slowly lumbering along. From ahead on the tracks came a raucous grinding sound as the engineer butted up against whatever barricade had been thrown up to stop the train.

"Keep shooting!" cried Spence, waving his S&W around wildly. Slocum wondered if the foreman had any idea how to use that hog-leg. It would have made him a mite happier if Spence had pointed the muzzle in the direction of the Indians.

"Golly, never heard of such a thing," Billy Buggs said, awestruck.

"What's that?"

"Injuns in these parts don't attack. Not like this. They're peaceable and have been for years and years." As if to gainsay Billy, several more chunks of hot lead ripped through the side of the passenger car, these carrying away both splinters and glass shards from the car's superstructure. Slocum poked his head up like a prairie dog looking for danger, spotted four more Indians high in trees alongside the tracks, and fired at them until his Colt Navy came up empty. Only then did he drop back and take the time to reload.

"Slocum, you got more ammo?" asked Spence, walking in a crouch along the aisle. Slocum saw the foreman had not fired even once.

"Got a little more. Not much," Slocum warned. He bobbed up and down fast, taking in the situation outside. The train strained to push through the barricade, but didn't seem to be doing a good job of it. Until the track was clear, they would be easy targets. The Indians weren't overly aggressive, as if they intended to wait for those inside the train to mosey out into their gun sights.

"We got to do something," Spence said.

"Yeah," Slocum said. He scuttled away from Spence and made his way forward, avoiding the men cowering under the seats. Coming to the door at the front of the car, Slocum pushed it open and drew some fire. When he heard the hammer on a distant rifle fall metallically, the magazine spent, he moved. Fast. Swarming out, he got his feet under him and jumped, scrambling to the top of the wood tender just in front of the passenger car. Keeping low, he made his way through the stacked wood in the tender and then dropped into the engine cab.

"Who are you?" demanded the engineer, crouched down behind a steel plate to protect himself from the sporadic gunfire from the woods on either side of the train.

"Get up a head of steam. When I give the signal, get the train moving."

"What are you going to do?" the engineer asked, but Slocum was already taking in the situation. Indians from back down the tracks were catching up with the train. Slocum didn't want them joining the few in the band who were trying to—do what? He couldn't figure out what the attack was supposed to accomplish. The train carried nothing more than a few men on their way to a lumbering camp. There might be something worth stealing in the two freight cars behind the passenger car, but the Indians weren't concentrating on opening the freight car doors.

He was damned if he could figure out what they were up to.

Slocum grabbed a slender piece of wood intended to feed the voracious steam boiler and stuffed only the end of it into the firebox. The dry wood ignited, and Slocum was on his way. He dropped to the ground, staying low, and went to the front of the train.

As he had thought, a few fallen tree trunks had been dragged over the tracks and secured with rope. The train could only push the trees along as it advanced. This changed fast when Slocum set fire to the ropes and the dried limbs. He jumped back as a blast of heat seared him. The Indians had not bothered to chop down a tree, but had relied on those already fallen and dried.

A bullet whined past his head, forcing him back into a crouch. Slocum spun about, aimed, and fired in a smooth motion. He was rewarded with an ear-piercing screech of pain. He had only winged the Indian, but it was enough to spook the others.

Slocum ran back to the engine cab and swung up.

"Get moving. The barricade's about burned through."

"It'll set us on fire!" protested the engineer. Then the man blanched when Slocum leveled his six-shooter and aimed it at him. The engineer kicked the firebox door shut and began twisting valves. Steam hissed and the powerful Baldwin engine shuddered. Then it seemed to leap forward as the barricade burned through. The train raced along the tracks at a breakneck pace, leaving the attacking Indians far behind.

"Sorry I lost my head," the engineer said. "You kin put that hunk of iron down now."

Slocum holstered his six-gun.

"This kind of thing happen often?" Slocum asked.

The engineer took off his striped cap and wiped his forehead, leaving behind dirty smudges. He shook his head.

"Cain't say it has. But them Injuns been kickin' up a big fuss lately. This is the first they shot me up, though." The engineer swallowed hard and leaned out the window at the side of the cab. "I sure hope they don't fire any of the bridges. There's one hundred fifteen of 'em along the route into the woods."

Slocum let out a low whistle. He had not realized this territory was so mountainous. Every bridge would have to be guarded—or at least checked before a train rumbled over it. If the Indians were serious about attacking the California Western trains, the advantage lay with them.

"What tribe did they belong to?" Slocum asked, remembering what Billy Buggs had said.

The engineer shook his head. "They all look the same to me, 'specially if they're sightin' along a rifle barrel with me in front. Don't get much trouble usually."

"Usually," Slocum said. He made his way back to the passenger car, looking both left and right of the tracks for any sign of more trouble. The Indians had given up. He dropped down and brushed himself off.

"That was real good work, Slocum," Spence said. The foreman pushed his bowler back and stared at him. Slocum wasn't sure what was going on in the man's mind. Mixed emotions flashed on his weathered face, and gratitude wasn't very prominent. Nor was relief. "Glad I hired you on."

"I try to earn my keep," Slocum said. The others in the car were brushing off glass from the seats and trying to present as small a profile as possible to any other Indian snipers. Slocum dropped back into his seat across from Billy Buggs.

"You're about the bravest man I ever seen," the youth said. "Even my pa's not up to fightin' an entire tribe of Indians."

Slocum shrugged it off. He leaned back and got an hour's sleep before the engine pulled into the lumbering camp. The odor of fragrant redwood sawdust came to him, as pure and sweet as biscuits cooking on a cold morning.

"We got to hike down the mountain to the camp," Spence said. He saw Slocum's interest and pointed. "That there's a three-hundred-foot-tall redwood. We cut down bigger ones, but not in this canyon."

"What do you do with it after it's downed?" Slocum asked.

"We have some steam donkeys up on top of the rise, near the railroad tracks, for ones that size. But the smaller ones we roll downhill to Pudding Creek and float all the way to Fort Bragg and the sawmill. Now shake a leg. We got trees to chop!"

The camp among the trees was larger than Slocum had suspected from the top of the ridge. There might be as many as a hundred men working for the company. Chinese cooks worked preparing food for the evening meal. Some washed and others tended small fires fed by limbs from the redwood trees, giving an even more pleasant scent to the camp. Slocum dropped his gunbelt and Colt Navy amid blankets given him by a sullen man at the company stores tent. He signed for the two blankets and a change of clothing, noting he was already in debt to C. R. Johnson's company for more than ten dollars. Slocum knew it could get worse.

Tent space was plentiful, as if many of the loggers had left. He picked a spot in one tent and immediately regretted it.

"Mind if I bunk with you, Mr. Slocum? Not that this is perzactly bunkin', mind you," said Billy Buggs.

Slocum shook his head. The loquacious youth was going to drive him to distraction.

"Spence is bellowing for us," Slocum said. "Let's go saw wood."

"Rather be sawing wood in my bunk, if you know

what I mean." Billy Buggs performed an exaggerated yawn, then laughed and joined Slocum.

"We got a crew of new men," Spence declared. "Even if you been lumberjacks all your born days, I'm putting you with men who've been here a spell." He paired up the newcomers and put them with crews already at work. Slocum and Billy trudged downhill and joined a team of men working down the side of the ridge.

"Glory be," Billy said, staring up at the tree the lumberjacks were impatiently sawing at with a crosscut saw. "How come they're so far up the trunk?" Billy peered as men on a platform cut into the tree almost fifteen feet above the forest floor. Slocum wondered the same thing, but wasn't going to ask.

"We don't cut lower 'cuz of the burls," one of the loggers said. "Hit one of them buggers and the saw bucks and breaks. You don't want that."

"No," said Billy. "Might cut the cutter."

"You catch on fast," the logger said. "There's another reason. Redwoods store a passel of water in the lower ten feet of their trunks. We try floatin' this one, and it'd sink like a stone."

"Isn't it big enough to wrestle uphill to the California Western for shipping?" asked Slocum. He shielded his eyes, trying to guess at the height. It was big, really big.

"Might, might not. Depends on how tall it is and how easy it'd be getting down to the river. We're mighty far down, and even using steam donkeys and them worthless Chinee in camp, it might not be possible to get it up to the railroad."

"Hey, Rufus, we almost got it through. Send somebody up to spell us, will you?" bellowed a man on the ledge above them.

"Time to get your feet wet," the one named Rufus

said. "Come on up. Spence tole me to wet-nurse you boys till you learn what you're doin'."

Rufus scrambled up the rope ladder like a monkey. Slocum followed more slowly, and Billy Buggs struggled with every rung. By the time he reached the platform cut into the side of the tree, Slocum and Rufus were already on one side of the long jagged-toothed saw.

"Grab hold. Lou'll work with you."

They set to sawing. Slocum watched as the sawdust exploded from their cut. The tree was a good ten feet thick and the big notch rose far above his head.

"How long before the tree falls?" he asked after they had been sawing for fifteen minutes.

Rufus laughed. "Gettin' tired? We got a ways to go. Another foot or better."

"I hear this crackin' sound," Billy said. "Like it's gettin' ready to break."

"You don't know nuthin', boy," Rufus said contemptuously. "We got another foot, minimum, to saw 'fore—"

The first crack sounded like a gunshot. Slocum looked up and saw the immense redwood tipping over as if it would fall on top of him. Then a second sound came, a noise louder than thunder in a spring rainstorm.

Slocum shoved Rufus back, but saw Billy Buggs was frozen where he stood on the platform, mouth wide open as he gawked at the slowly falling tree. His partner on the saw had already dived off the platform, hitting the ground hard.

The thunder sounded again. Louder. Then the redwood jerked as if it had been shot out of a cannon, the butt end snapping back and down as the redwood started its long fall to the forest floor.

Slocum dug in his toes and dived, tackling Billy and driving him back out of the way of the kicking stump end of the redwood. Slocum felt a blow like that of an ax handle across his back. Then he was falling through the air, hanging onto a struggling Billy Buggs.

They crashed to the ground, and the world went dark around Slocum.

"He's gonna be all right. Git back and give the man some air," growled Rufus.

Slocum blinked and tried to puzzle out what he saw. Blues and greens and browns. When he realized he was staring through tree limbs at the sky, everything came rushing back to him.

"Billy?"

"The little snot's got a busted arm. Spence decided to send him on back to Fort Bragg. You got anything busted up inside?"

Slocum took a deep breath. No sharp pain, only aches. He sat up, forcing away the spinning world around him.

"Reckon I'm still in one piece. What happened?"

"You done saved Rufus, that's what," said Lou. "And the kid too."

"The tree snapped off premature-like," Rufus explained. "Didn't know part of it was rotted through."

Slocum looked past the small knot of lumberjacks and saw that the tree had tumbled downhill in the direction of the creek. The end had broken when they had reached the critical point, and snapped, kicking back unexpectedly. They all could have been killed.

"You saved me havin' to go fetch more men, Slocum," said Spence's voice. Slocum struggled to focus on the foreman. "This is twice today you did the Fort Bragg Lumber Company a good turn. Just don't go expectin' any reward for it. We all stick together out here in the woods."

"Not asking for anything," Slocum said, getting to his

feet. He stood and then fell heavily, his right leg refusing to support him. Pain lanced through his hip and made him grunt.

"What's wrong? I didn't think he'd busted anything like the kid."

Slocum was glad Spence had not gone into doctoring. His bedside manner left much to be desired. Slocum ran his hands along his thigh and winced again as pain racked him.

"Hurts like hell."

"Lemme check it out," Rufus said. "We don't have a doc in camp, so whatever I say goes." He looked around to see if Spence disagreed. The foreman shook his head and moved on, shouting orders to get the limbs off the felled redwood so it could be dragged downhill to the river for transport to Fort Bragg.

"You give me a real twinge every time you press there," Slocum said. "But it doesn't feel like a broken bone."

"Not broken, just bruised as all get-out," Rufus said. "I'll talk to Spence. If you rest up for a day or two, you'll be good as new. You got a bad bruise, that's all. Might be a sprain, though I never seen one that high up, 'cept when Knut Jenssen went to a San Francisco whorehouse and took on all the ladies there in a single night. And then it wasn't his leg what went hurtin'!"

Rufus argued with Spence a few minutes, then came back to help Slocum to camp.

"He's a mean cuss. Wanted to send you back to Fort Bragg along with the kid. I talked him out of it, me and Lou. We can surely use men with your good sense and fast reactions," Rufus said. They made their way up the hill, Slocum grimacing with every step.

"Jist flop on down and you'll be good as gold in a day or two," Rufus assured him. He turned and stopped at the tent where two Chinese men stood, peering in. "Git your yellow asses out of my way." Rufus back-handed one, who dodged the blow expertly. The other made way for the logger.

The two Celestials spoke to one another in their sing-song language, then started to leave, but Slocum called to them.

"Hold on," Slocum said. "I've heard tell you know about herbs and poultices. I bruised my leg. Can you fix me up?"

The two looked at each other, then held a long conversation with each other behind their raised hands.

"You talkee to Chinee boy?" asked one.

"Why not?" Slocum had seen how they were treated, and it didn't sit well with him. "You work for the lumber company or the railroad?"

"We not build railroad," one said. "We washee, washee."

"Can you do anything for my leg?" he repeated. Again the pair held a long conversation. Then the one who had narrowly avoided Rufus's slap motioned.

Slocum gritted his teeth and hobbled along behind them. As they made their way through the camp, he saw a half-dozen Indians lounging around. When one spat at the Celestials as they passed, Slocum stopped and faced the Indian.

"You got a problem?" he asked.

"You yellow like them?" demanded the Indian, standing up and thrusting out his chest belligerently. "I treat them like white man treat them." The Indian went to spit on the Chinese again, only to end up gurgling when Slocum's strong hand clamped on the man's throat. Slocum squeezed and lifted.

"You calling me yellow? I'd rather be like them than you. What do you do around here?"

"Plenty," grated the Indian, struggling to breathe. "I—"

"Let him go, sir," said a cold voice. "There is no call to harm him."

Slocum turned and saw about the prettiest woman he had ever seen standing behind him. The look of pure venom in her eyes did nothing to rob her of her beauty.

He released the Indian, who went scuttling off muttering dire threats as he vanished into the forest.

3

"You should learn manners. Most everyone in this horrible camp ought to learn to be more civilized. How dare you treat that poor Indian in such a fashion!" The woman's blue eyes sparked with fire matching her bright coppery hair as it caught the light slanting down through the tall redwoods.

"I was trying to teach *him* manners," Slocum said, still angry. He did not doubt the white men in the camp treated the Chinese exactly the way the Indian had tried to. It didn't make much difference to him who he backed down from such behavior. He wasn't going to tolerate it, even in this pretty woman.

"I shall see that you are dismissed," she said.

"No man spits on another. I'd say your manners are the ones needing some sprucing up."

"What?" she raged. She even stamped her foot. Slocum saw he had caught her attention, and that was fine. He wanted to find out why she thought it was all right to torment the Celestials.

"You think it's all right for an Indian to spit on a Chinaman. I don't—"

"What are you talking about? You were beating up that poor . . ." The woman's voice trailed off as she looked to the Chinese men gathered around them. Many were nodding in Slocum's direction. One shuffled forward, hands hidden in padded sleeves.

"Sir, please, I make poultice for you. Thank you. Chan does not speak your language so good." Again came the bow. "It is his mistake to allow the red heathen to spit on him."

"You were—" the woman said. Again she stopped as she looked around and read the truth of the matter in the gathered Chinamen's usually impassive faces.

"My name's Slocum and you can go tell Spence you're firing me. I want a day's pay, especially after saving two men from getting themselves killed." Slocum looked at the man who had been called Chan and added, "And I reckon I saved another from being humiliated for no good reason other than cruelty."

"I believe I owe you an apology, Mr. Slocum," the woman admitted. "This matter deserves more careful scrutiny. There are so many of the Indians who hang about the camp begging for handouts. Only a few prove themselves useful, doing occasional chores."

"Ma'am," Slocum said. "I don't want to stay anywhere where the hired help's treated so bad. The way I look at it, I'm hired help around here too. So you just go on and get me fired."

"Please, sir. This is a misunderstanding. My name's Faith Gaynor, and my father is Ed Gaynor, Mr. Johnson's vice president and acting superintendent for the camp and sawmill. Mr. Johnson spends so much time back East it is necessary for someone to be present, either here or back in Fort Bragg."

"So your pa's the real boss around here? Hadn't heard Spence mention him."

"Spence," Faith said, venting a sigh. "He can be such a trial at times."

Slocum had no idea what the redhead meant by that, and he wasn't inclined to ask. His thigh muscle throbbed painfully and swelled, threatening to rip the tough canvas fabric of his jeans. He hobbled over to a tree and used it for support.

"Get you fine poultice," the Celestial said. "Help bruise." The man bobbed his head up and down.

"I'm game," Slocum said. "Anything to stop the pain."

"Let me help you over to my cabin," Faith said to Slocum. The Celestial bobbed his head a few times to show he understood, bowed, and backed away. The woman put her arm around Slocum and guided him toward a cabin nestled at the edge of the forest. Slocum tried not to have her support much of his weight, but every yard he walked took that much more out of him. By the time they reached the cabin door, a red curtain of pain was closing in on him.

He sank to the top step leading up into the cabin and leaned back to catch his breath.

"Thanks for the help. I'm not used to hurting this bad."

"I can see the muscle pulsating," Faith said, almost in awe. Gentle fingers traced over the huge bulge on Slocum's thigh. Her touch was appreciated, but when she probed, he gritted his teeth to keep from calling out. "That is a serious injury. You got it helping others?"

"Tree broke while we were sawing on it. Pushed Rufus out of the way and then knocked another fella to the ground. Broke his arm but saved his life."

"Logging is a dangerous business," Faith said, continuing her examination. She looked up and brushed a strand of copper-colored hair from her eyes when she saw a Chinaman hurrying in their direction.

"Put this on leg. Heal day or two," the Celestial said,

bowing repeatedly. "I make special when Chan tell me what happened. This work good."

"Thanks," Slocum said. "I need to get to my tent over yonder." He blinked, and realized he couldn't focus his eyes. The pain was welling up and choking off both vision and rational thought. He had been shot, he had had broken bones, he had been burned and trampled by angry longhorns, but never had he experienced this kind of unrelenting pain.

"Nonsense," Faith said. "Help me get him into my cabin, Li. That's why we came over here, after all." She and the Chinaman helped Slocum inside and laid him on the comfortable bed. Slocum heard scissors snipping, and felt almost immediate relief when Faith cut away his pants leg and released the swollen flesh underneath.

"The pressure was hurting me something fierce," he said. "I can—" He almost passed out when the China-man began slathering on the slimy poultice. Pain rock-eted through his body and exploded in his brain. Slocum might have lost consciousness, but wasn't sure.

The next thing he knew Faith was laying a damp com-press on his head. Cool air blew past his bare leg, save where the poultice had been applied.

"The pain's not so bad now," he said in wonder.

"Li says you should not put any weight on it for an-other few hours."

"I need to get back to my tent then."

"Why?" Faith asked, her eyes wide and innocent. She seemed oblivious to the rumors that would start if any of the perpetually horny lumberjacks should find she was nursing him in her cabin—alone. The Celestial was no-where to be seen.

"Your pa's not likely to cotton much to me being here alone with you."

"Nothing untoward will happen," Faith said primly. "Besides, I can fend off any advance you might make." She playfully slapped his leg. The lance of white-hot pain caused Slocum to arch his back and writhe about on the bed.

"Oh, Mr. Slocum, I'm *sorry*. I was only being playful. I didn't mean to hurt you further."

"The poultice, whatever's in it, works good," Slocum said. "The pain's going away again."

They settled down, Faith sitting on the edge of the bed and Slocum lying uncomfortably, not sure what to say. He finally broke the silence.

"Any injuries from the attack on the train?"

"What are you talking about?" Faith seemed genuinely horrified when he told her about the Indian attack on the train from Fort Bragg.

"Father never mentioned it. Neither did Spence. They don't want to worry me, but this kind of thing is happening more and more. We used to get along quite well with the Indians, but something has stirred them up of late."

"It's only recently the Pomo have begun their attacks?"

"The Pomo? I suppose it is them. That was a Pomo you choked. They have been quite content to do odd jobs. I cannot imagine what has gotten into them to go around burning bridges and attacking trains like this."

"So there've been other attacks?" Slocum asked.

"A few." Faith sighed heavily, causing her breasts to rise and fall delightfully under her crisp white blouse. "I hear snippets, but Father tries to keep it from me. And Spence *never* talks of such things. With him it is always business, cut here, move there."

Slocum lay back and wondered what was going on. The Pomo had been peaceable enough, even docile, until recently. Whatever had stirred the ones who had attacked had not run through every member of their tribe like wildfire, not if the Indian he had run off was any indication. Some were still willing to mingle with the white men cutting down their forests.

"It sounds as if Father might want me back in Fort Bragg, out of danger. I don't know why the threat should be increasing, but it seems to be."

"The camp's pretty well-established," Slocum observed. "Any talk of moving into a different part of the forest for the logging?"

"We're always moving up the canyons. That's where the redwoods grow, you know. They suck in the fog as well as the rain, which can be quite sparse this far inland."

Slocum had never given it much thought, but a huge tree needed a considerable amount of water. The waxy, tough fronds on the redwood must suck up the moisture from the seemingly perpetual fog infesting the lower reaches of the mountains.

"Anyone ever hurt in the camp from Indian attacks?" Slocum asked.

The woman shook her head. A curl of red hair snaked down over her forehead. She was hardly aware of the quick, nervous toss of her head that got it back in place.

"What do you do out here?" Slocum asked.

"Why, I keep books. I approve supply orders and see to it that the arriving mail is dispensed and the letters written by the men sent back to the coast. The job keeps me quite busy."

"No time off at all?" Slocum asked.

Faith stared at him and a tiny smile came to her lips. "What did you have in mind?" she asked boldly.

A sharp rap at the cabin door diverted their attention. Before Faith could say a word, the door opened and a well-dressed man pushed in. He was graying, and from the way he played with his pince-nez, nearsighted.

"My dear, do you have the supply list ready yet? The train will be departing soon." The man peered through the spectacles at Slocum and Faith. He drew himself up a little taller and pulled back his shoulders. Slocum made him to be about six feet tall but carrying more suet than muscle under his fancy duds. Not fat perhaps, but there was a softness to him that spoke of the city and not the hard life of the lumberjack.

"Father, this is Mr. Slocum. He was injured and I was ministering to him."

Ed Gaynor looked with some disapproval at Slocum.

"I don't believe I know you, sir," Gaynor said.

"Mr. Slocum is a new logger, just come in on the train—the one that was *attacked*," Faith said. "Why did you keep it from me, Father?"

Gaynor harrumphed and said, "Slocum? You the one who saved the train? Spence mentioned you. I believe the boy returning to Fort Bragg did also. You saved his life, I believe."

"It's been a long day," Slocum allowed.

"Well, yes," Gaynor said, unsure of himself. He cleared his throat again. "I see that your injury is not a serious one. My daughter is a good nurse, but she has other chores in the camp. Yes, other duties to tend to. And there's Spence."

"Oh, Father," Faith said, exasperated. Slocum caught something of the byplay between them, but couldn't fill in the details. He had the hollow feeling there was something between Faith and the camp foreman. No matter how obliging Spence might feel toward Slocum for saving lives and pulling his fat out of the fire on the train ride up from the coast, he wasn't likely to approve of Slocum cutting in on his girl.

"I can get back to my tent," Slocum said.

"That is a smelly unguent," Gaynor said, peering down at Slocum's leg. "What is it?"

"Don't rightly know. Li fixed it up for me."

"Li? One of the Celestials? I did not realize they knew how to do anything but the laundry."

"Father," Faith said, looking quickly from Slocum to her father, "there seems so much going on that we don't understand. Perhaps we should do something about it."

"What do you mean, my dear?"

Faith bit her lower lip before speaking. "The Pomo are turning fiercer, if they attack our trains. There was that bridge-burning incident last week also."

"It was nothing. Only an accident, I am sure." The way Gaynor spoke he was anything but sure.

"Two Indians were seen nearby. I spoke to the train engineer. That was the freight train bringing our supplies. We might have been cut off for weeks if the trestle had been burned."

"What are you getting at, Faith?"

"Father, we need to know what is going on. Spence isn't telling us."

"He probably doesn't know any more than we do," Gaynor said. "I still don't see what you're suggesting."

"Mr. Slocum is going to be laid up for a few more days. Why not let him poke about and see what he can find about the Pomo? If there are problems, perhaps we can speak with them and nip this violence in the bud."

"They always seem amenable to a meal or two when they come into camp," Gaynor said distantly. "We've never turned them away. In fact, we treat them just like white men."

"They've certainly adopted some of our traits," Slocum said carefully, remembering how the Indian had belittled the Chinaman. "Miss Gaynor had not mentioned this to me, but I'd be willing. I'm a good tracker and might find out what's eating at the Pomo before any big trouble erupts."

"Hmm, yes, perhaps so. Your leg's not going to trouble you?"

"I'll be able to walk just fine in an hour or two. The poultice is working fine."

"Very well. I'll tell Spence you're laid up for a day or two. He listens to me. I'm superintendent, after all. You find what you can, Slocum. I must have that supply list soon, Faith. There's something more to do, but I can't remember what it was. Oh, yes, the new saw blades. Broke two this week. Find what type Spence needs and get them from our supplier in Fort Bragg."

Muttering to himself, Gaynor left his daughter's cabin.

"I knew this would work out for the best, Mr. Slocum," Faith gushed. "You can discover what is wrong with the Pomo and put an end to their depredations. We are reasonable people. We can help them if they are in trouble. Oh, this is so good!" Faith enthused.

Slocum wasn't so sure, but she was a pretty sight, the way her face glowed with innocence and hope.

In an hour he left her cabin, and in three, just after chuck, Slocum was walking well enough to make his way from camp and into the woods. He went slowly, picking his way along a game trail that showed signs of having more than one moccasin print on it.

Slocum wished he had some idea where the Pomo camp might be, but if it took all night to find it he wasn't going to complain. He preferred the freedom and solitude of the forest to the bustling lumber camp. More than that, not rubbing elbows with the other loggers made this foray worthwhile. It gave him time to think about the train attack, of what he might learn about the Pomo, and about Faith Gaynor.

Mostly Slocum thought of the lovely red-haired woman with the flashing blue eyes and impetuous manner. She seemed out of place in the forest, a gem in the wilderness.

As he made his way along the trail, Slocum slowly became aware of a new scent in the air. He got off the trail and turned, sniffing hard at the cool night breeze.

Woodsmoke.

He left the trail and cut through dense undergrowth, trying not to blunder along like some tenderfoot but finding the going hard because of his gimpy leg. There was no light, from either the half-moon or the stars, sneaking under the tall mantle of the towering spruce and redwoods. Worse, his leg was beginning to throb again. He needed more of the herb poultice to quell the pain.

The sound of men ahead forced Slocum to slow even more. Then he flopped onto his belly and wiggled through the forest to a spot where he spied on an Indian camp. Two dozen Indians sat around a large fire, now turning to embers. He had no way of knowing if they were Pomo or some other tribe. More to the point, he had no idea if they were the warriors who had attacked the train.

None wore war paint, but many worked on their rifles and carefully sharpened arrowheads as they sat around the fire. One man began singing, but Slocum did not recognize the lingo. Perhaps they were Pomo, but they might be some other tribe out on a hunting expedition. Perhaps they were the Indians responsible for the attacks on the logging camp, with Gaynor and Spence simply mistaking them for Pomo.

He had a lot to learn before he returned to camp.

An hour of lying in hiding wore on Slocum. His leg provided a constant source of annoyance, a dull ache rather than sharp pain, but with enough discomfort to keep him distracted. Slocum wondered how long he might have to snoop before he figured out if he had found something worthwhile. The Indians appeared to be peaceable enough, even if they kept their weapons close at hand.

The creaking of a bow as its string pulled back caused him to roll to his side and look behind him. A short Indian stood there, arrow nocked and drawn taut. If Slocum moved a muscle, the arrow would fly straight and true to his heart.

4

"You smell," the Indian said, wrinkling his nose. "And you spy on us."

"I didn't mean anything by it," Slocum lied. His mind raced. He wasn't in any position to draw his six-shooter, and he sure as hell couldn't outrun the brave with the arrow aimed squarely at him. All the Indian had to do was release the string and the arrow would end Slocum's life.

"We have nothing to steal," the Indian said.

This told Slocum he wasn't likely to have blundered into the camp of the Indians responsible for the attacks on the logging camp and the railroad supplying it. They would be more interested in stealing than being robbed.

"I hurt my leg," Slocum said, pointing at his right thigh. "I hoped you might be of some help. I can't walk too good."

"Spying on us doesn't get you any help," said another Indian from the camp. He towered over Slocum, a rifle cradled in the crook of his left arm. The Indian looked to the first brave and nodded. The man with the bow and arrow vanished back into the night. Slocum didn't even hear the soft whisper of the brave's moccasins as he moved across the leaf- and needle-strewn forest floor.

"I was saying that—"

"Lies, all lies. That is what we expect from you," the Indian said. There was less disgust in his tone than resignation, as if he expected only new lies and never the truth from any white man he came across, even one hiding in the forest spying on his band. The warrior inclined his head in the direction of the dying campfire. He lifted his rifle just enough to tell Slocum it wasn't a friendly invitation to join their party.

Wincing as he put weight on his gimpy leg, Slocum made his way to the wan heat of the fire. He rubbed his hands and warmed them as he looked around, trying not to seem too obvious. Outrunning the Indians was out of the question. He couldn't get to the edge of their camp before they filled him with lead and arrows. Once in the forest, he stood little chance of evading them.

That they hadn't plugged him outright was a good sign. Slocum remembered some advice he had gotten once from a Confederate colonel. "When you're in a hole, son," the officer had said, "the first thing you do is stop digging."

Slocum cleared his throat and then said loud enough for all to hear, "I was looking for the warriors who tried to rob the California Western Railroad today."

This caused the leader of the band to recoil slightly. He wasn't used to such honesty from white men. The Indians exchanged sideways glances and more than one of them shrugged, as if unheeding of such concerns.

"We do not rob your trains. They are smelly, worse than angry skunks. They make too much noise and scare away the game. But we do not try to rob them." He crouched down by the fire and warmed his hands. Slocum settled down to the ground beside him, saying nothing. There was an etiquette dealing with Indians he often wished white men would adopt. When the leader of the

Indians had had his say, he would expect Slocum to respond—but not before.

A few minutes later, the Indian continued.

"The game becomes scarce and hunting is harder. We move inland, away from the men who cut trees."

"Are you of the Pomo tribe?" Slocum asked. If they weren't responsible for the attempted robbery, perhaps they knew others—renegades—in their tribe who were guilty.

"Pomo?" The leader laughed and spoke rapidly. Slocum heard the name "Pomo" several more times. This produced a new round of merriment from the gathered Indians. He couldn't figure what they found so funny until the leader explained.

"What do you call this?" The Indian poked at a rock.

"A rock."

"It is not like that rock," the leader said, pointing across the campsite to another, "yet you call it a rock too."

"You're saying not all Indians are Pomo?"

This produced another laugh. The Indian shook his head and smiled.

"I am saying we are all Pomo, no matter what the tribe. It means no more than 'the People.' And we are all *the* People." He laughed again while Slocum digested this information.

"You're saying all the Indians along the coast, no matter what their actual tribe, call themselves Pomo?"

The man nodded. Slocum realized his chore had expanded. Spence and the others at the Fort Bragg Lumber Company camp had no idea who had attacked. They had applied the name Pomo to those responsible. They might as well have called them Indians, for all the information that carried.

"Do you know of a tribe fighting the white men at the logging camp?" Slocum asked.

The leader shrugged. "If I did, I would not tell you. You think to capture them and take them to hang. A man who dies with a rope around his neck is forever barred from the Happy Lands and is forced to walk this world as a ghost." He shivered, and Slocum knew it wasn't from the cold. Many tribes feared ghosts, from the Navajos to the Walapai and on to the coast, where the Pomo did also.

Pomo. The People.

"I will not let those responsible for the robberies be hanged," Slocum promised. "A bullet only, so they can die in battle."

"That is good. I would rather die in bed with my two wives," the man said, laughing.

"You have nothing to fear if you are not the ones responsible," Slocum said.

"We have nothing to fear because we leave the coast and go to the holy mountain."

Slocum reckoned the Indian meant Mt. Shasta.

Slocum fell silent and waited, wondering what they would do with him. He still had his six-shooter, so he could take a few of them with him if they tried to kill him. Still, he saw no way of getting away alive if they chose to push the matter.

His belly grumbled and squatting down cramped his bruised leg. The muscle gave him the twinges, but Slocum did not move. The Indians were in control of the situation.

"You hunt these robbers?" asked the leader of the warriors after several minutes of silent thought.

"That's all," Slocum answered.

"Then go hunt them. Let us hunt for deer and bear. We leave the coast peacefully."

Slocum silently stood, got his leg under him, and walked into the forest. Every hair on his neck twitched in expectation of an arrow or rifle bullet crashing into his back. The darkness swallowed him, slowing his progress even more than his aching leg. Slocum knew he had a tendency to circle to the right if he was not careful, so he forced himself to swing left at every opportunity. He eventually found a game trail. It might have been the one he'd followed earlier or another. He couldn't tell in the dark.

Only when he found shelter in the hollowed-out trunk of a huge redwood did he rest a little easier. The hunters he had blundered onto were not the ones causing the ruckus. If anything, they sought the same thing Ed Gaynor did: to be left alone.

Slocum slept fitfully, his arms wrapped tightly around himself to conserve warmth. He awoke with a start, hand flashing to the Colt Navy in his cross-draw holster when two distant gunshots rang out. Slocum blinked and then rubbed his eyes, realizing he had slept longer than he had planned. Dim morning light worked its liquid warmth through the forest canopy and brought day to the forest.

Another gunshot got him to his feet. His leg was stiff but no longer hurting the way it had. The Chinese potion had worked a miracle on his bruised muscle.

Slocum swiveled about, trying to locate the source of the gunfire. He remembered something else his old Confederate commander had told him: "Don't kick a fresh turd on a hot day." Whatever went on in the forest was none of his business. Staying clear of men shooting at each other meant he was less likely to end up with a slug in his gut.

"Hunters," Slocum said softly to himself. They might be hunters, but he did not think so. When four more quick shots echoed through the trees, he knew he wasn't hearing the result of a careful hunt. This was a gunfight.

"Yee-aaieee!" came the ear-splitting screech from his left. Slocum ducked back into the hollowed redwood trunk, his six-gun out and ready for action. It took only a few seconds before the man making the sound came running pell-mell along the path.

Scrawny to the point of emaciation, a frightened look on his face, the Indian ran faster than Slocum would have thought possible for any human being. Short legs pumping, the man ran past where Slocum hid, never seeing him. It took Slocum a few seconds to realize the man was armed only with a knife. Whoever had fired the shots was chasing this Indian.

The band of Indians appearing on the man's heels obviously intended to kill anyone they found. Five of them waved their rifles around, occasionally firing into the brush to spook anything—or anyone—hiding there. They moved quickly, but Slocum figured their quarry would be in the next county before they caught up. They moved fast; he was flat out running.

Slipping back into the trunk of the redwood, Slocum watched as the Indian warriors stalked past. They sported war paint, but Slocum could not identify their tribe.

Pomo, he thought to himself, amused at the notion that all the Indians called themselves "the People."

Slocum tensed when one of the Indians stopped a few yards from him. The man put his nose into the air and sniffed hard, turning slowly. Slocum remembered he had been discovered before by the heavy odor from the poultice on his leg. But the Indian kept turning and motioned to the others with him to continue down the trail.

It wasn't Slocum's fight, and he had only woe to gain if he intervened, but he couldn't help himself. Curiosity

compelled him to trail the Indians on the trail of the
skinny brave running along so fast and frightened. He
started after the five hunting for the scrawny Indian, only
to find the trail curling about through the forest and going downhill. Within a few hundred yards, Slocum entered a fog so thick he could hardly see a dozen feet
ahead.

He slowed and then stopped, deciding it wasn't worth
his neck to continue and perhaps blunder into the five
armed braves. He swiped at the clammy moisture bead-
ing on his face and tried to look up into the trees, remembering what Faith had told him. The fog might be
good for the redwoods but it was hell for him.

Slocum turned, and had begun retracing his path when
he heard more gunshots. The fog muffled the report. He
shook his head, knowing this wasn't his fight.

Barely had he started back up the trail when he heard
the distinctive thud-thud-thud of moccasins on the
ground. Slocum stepped off the dirt footpath and let the
scrawny Indian run past. The man had successfully doubled back on his pursuers, but failed to see Slocum in
his hurry to escape.

Slocum trailed the Indian until the fog lightened. He
looked for someplace to hole up until the back-and-forth
chase was over. Tangling with one band of Indians was
enough for him. Barely had Slocum climbed back out
of the gently drifting fingers of fog when he saw something that turned him cold inside.

Ahead, in a clearing where sunlight shone on her like
a lantern, stood Faith Gaynor. She waved frantically, and
Slocum thought she was signaling him until he stepped
out of the fog. Her gaze wasn't fixed on him but on the
fleeing Indian.

"This way. You can hide here!" The woman pointed

to a tangle of undergrowth off the trail. She rushed ahead of the man, showing him the way.

Slocum dropped to the ground and lay quietly in the weeds when he heard the five hunters coming back up the trail. Whatever their quarry had done to confuse his trail had been deciphered. Only now the five armed and angry Indians were after not just the man, but Faith Gaynor as well.

"What's she doing out here?" Slocum grumbled as the last of the Indians ran past him, traveling faster than the wind and gusting by him as obliviously. He pushed himself to his hands and knees, then stood. His leg gave him some trouble again, but he thrust the pain out of his mind. Letting those five catch up with their prey was one thing. Turning Faith over to them was something else. He knew nothing of why they chased the solitary brave, but none of the five would take kindly to a white woman interfering with their vengeance. Slocum had come into the forest to find the Pomo responsible for attacking the train.

For all he knew, these five were the ones responsible. And they were about to capture a woman who knew next to nothing about hiding her tracks through a forest.

"Even if she did," Slocum muttered, "there's not enough time to cover her tracks properly."

The Indians out-legged him easily. Worse, even hurrying along, they were not put off the trail by anything either Faith or the man she succored did. The small band of Indians vanished into the woods, hot on the heels of their quarry.

More gunshots, a shriek of pain, and then silence. Slocum limped along the game trail, worrying about Faith. Then the worry turned to outright fear for her safety when a woman's high-pitched scream cut through the still forest. The sound vanished fast, swallowed by fog and vegetation, only to be replaced by men's throaty laughter.

Laughter signaling triumph.

5

Slocum's heart skipped a beat when deathly silence fell in the sequoia forest. The fog drifted up from downhill, circling his feet and face, mingling with the sudden sweat on his face. His hand brushed the ebony butt of his Colt Navy as he felt himself tossed on the horns of a dilemma.

If he returned to camp to get help, he might never find his way back to this clearing. Worse, he might return directly and find Faith's body riddled with bullet holes. Worst of all, he might find her alive but cruelly used by the Indians. They'd had the look of men intent on killing and mayhem. Finding the lovely redhead would be nothing more than a lagniappe to their deadly mission of killing their skinny quarry.

But if Slocum blundered onto them now, could he fight off five fit, angry warriors? His leg throbbed with a dull pain that threatened to explode into full-blown agony. Or was that only his indecision? He was not a man to deliberate. Slocum was a man of action.

The consequences flashed through his mind, and he ignored them. His six-shooter slid easily from his holster as he stalked forward, the fog trailing behind him like ghostly wisps of good sense.

The clearing quickly turned to dense forest within a hundred yards. Slocum advanced slowly, listening hard. His leg didn't bother him as much as it had before. Being decisive had focused him. Slocum sniffed the air, hunting for any hint of the Indians. He caught a faint whiff of violet.

Faith Gaynor had worn violet-scented toilet water when she tended him in her cabin.

Turning, he caught indistinct sounds of struggle deeper in the forest. Working his way through the dense tangle of underbrush produced a little noise that might betray him should any of the Indians be listening. Slocum doubted they were.

Fifteen minutes of fighting off the brambles and blackberry thorns brought him to another clearing. Slocum crouched and studied the grassy open area in front of him. He heaved a sigh when he saw a piece of gaudy cloth caught on a nearby twig. Making his way to it, Slocum pulled it free and looked at it. Faith's skirt had ripped as she came—or ran—this way.

He looked for any trace of blood and found none. That meant she was still unharmed. Slocum knew that wouldn't last long if the five warriors got to their camp.

Circling the clearing was the smartest thing he could do if the Indians watched their back trail or doubled around. But the leg that had been cooperating before now sent tiny needles of pain throughout his thigh and worked its way into his gut. Slocum set out directly across the clearing, exposed and vulnerable to an ambusher. Every step he took might bring him closer to the sniper who would prove to be his killer.

Sweat running down his face, he reached the far side of the clearing without being found out. Slocum leaned against a tree, weaker than a newborn kitten. He sank to the ground, a big redwood trunk at his back. Resting,

Slocum wiped more sweat from his face. Fever stalked him too. How he wished for some more of Li's strangely effective, smelly poultice for his leg. Or something for the mounting fever.

Crawling, then getting to his feet, Slocum stumbled on, wondering if he was even headed in the right direction. The path wound around the side of the hill, going lower into the canyon below. The sound of running water came to torment him. Slocum again found himself caught between pursuing Faith and her captors and getting water.

"Water," he decided. Without it, he could never go on. Slocum stumbled and fell to his knees at the edge of the rapidly running river. A creek they called such a narrow, deep river in these parts. He splashed water on his face and felt better for it. Then he drank his fill and felt the fever receding a mite.

"Gotta go on, but wanna rest," he said almost deliriously. Slocum collapsed by the stream and slept until the sun warmed the side of his face. He shook himself, feeling better, and drank more water. Peering through the trees, he wondered if he could possibly have slept away most of the day.

A quick look at his pocket watch convinced him that he had. Disgust at such weakness spurred him on. Slocum followed the creek for a few minutes and then worked higher, almost stumbling onto the Indians' camp without realizing it.

He stepped back and slipped behind a tree, waiting for the outcry from the camp. It never came. Slocum ventured a quick look around the trunk of the spruce and saw the Indians sleeping. The one who had been posted as sentry sat with his head resting on his knees, as sound asleep as the others.

Slocum saw his chance and knew he had to take it.

Heart pounding, he moved around the camp until he found the spot where the Indians had tied up their captives. The skinny Indian had been staked out spread-eagle and gagged with a thin piece of rawhide circling his head and savagely pulled back so his face was frozen into a permanent grimace. Slocum neither knew nor cared what this brave had done to anger the others. His eyes were on Faith and Faith alone.

The woman was bound to a stake nearer the five sleeping Indians. She was gagged and a thin piece of rawhide circled her slender throat, the other end fastened to a stake. Her hands were bound behind her back, with another short length of rawhide running from her wrists to one exposed ankle. If she tried to stand, she would strangle herself. But with her hands fastened so securely to one foot, Faith could hardly get that far.

The staked-out Indian turned his head and stared wide-eyed at Slocum. Faith had yet to see him. For that Slocum was glad. If she stirred, she might wake up the Indians nearest her.

The sun was setting and the forest turned chillier by the minute. Slocum was worried that this would awaken the Indians. They would get hungry and start a cooking fire. They would want the warmth of their blankets. The rising wind might stir them. Everything about the forest would work against him unless he acted fast.

On his belly, Slocum snaked toward the Indian captive. He needed help rescuing Faith, and the other prisoner was the only likely source of aid.

"Help me free the woman, and I'll get you out of here in one piece. You agree to help?" Slocum whispered in the Indian's ear.

The man nodded vigorously, but Slocum had expected that. Any hope of escape would be greeted with false promises of help.

Slocum moved closer and grabbed the stake holding the man's left hand. Tugging hard, Slocum found that the stake refused to budge. He wondered if he was weaker than he thought, the victim of his leg injury and fever, or if the angle was wrong. Slocum dared to come to his knees to get better leverage.

The dusk masked him enough to keep from being seen when the Indian on guard stretched, yawned, and glanced in the direction of the captive.

Slocum froze, waited until the sentry turned away, then sank back to the ground. He whispered to the bound Indian, "I'll be back. Count on it."

He slithered back into the bushes where he could hide and watch anxiously. The sentry had awakened only seconds before the others. Hunger and the need for warmth brought them from their sleep, as Slocum had feared. He stretched out flat on his belly and knew he had a considerable wait ahead. But patience was one of his virtues. During the war he had been a sniper—and one of the best the Confederacy had. Slocum remembered how he had often found a place, be it on a hilltop or in the crook of a tree, where he'd waited for long hours for a single shot. He had hunted for the glint of sunlight off an officer's braid before firing.

An army without its commanders was like a body without a head.

Slocum wished it was that easy now. Kill the leader of this war party and the other four would still come after him—or butcher Faith. This was a battle that had to be won by stealth and not by a single accurate shot. He watched as the cooking fire blazed merrily and the Indians ate heartily of fish they had found in the nearby creek. The aroma of cooking food made Slocum's mouth water and his belly growl.

He waited.

The Indian nearest Faith reached out and ran his fingers along her cheek. The woman recoiled, and Slocum aimed directly for the Indian's head. Slocum relaxed when the Indian laughed and left Faith alone. For the moment.

Slocum waited some more.

The five sat in a circle around the campfire, talking in low voices. Slocum wished he knew what they were plotting, but the chance of him knowing what dialect they spoke was small. He could get by in a dozen different lingoes, and make himself understood using sign language with just about any tribe on the Plains. But here?

He waited.

The cooking fire died down. The Indians pulled their blankets around their shoulders and soon slept again. Another had been posted as guard. He was more active than the former, getting up and strolling over to the spread-eagled Indian captive to kick him in the ribs a few times. Then the Indian checked Faith's bonds.

He almost died when he reached down and grabbed at her breasts. Slocum carefully lowered the hammer on his six-shooter again when the Indian laughed and walked off, making a wide circuit of the camp. Ten minutes later, he returned, satisfied they were safe.

In twenty minutes this sentry was sound asleep. Slocum made his move then. He retraced the snakelike path to the side of the bound Indian.

"Don't make a sound," Slocum whispered. "They're asleep, but if they hear us . . ." He let the captive come to his own conclusion about what the penalty for drawing attention would be.

Slocum struggled and tugged and pushed, finally getting the left stake free. The man's arm lifted up and sent the stake, still attached by a cord, flailing through the air. Slocum grabbed the man's arm and pulled it back.

"Settle down," he cautioned. Slocum worked to get the rawhide off the man's wrist. The flesh had turned purple where the cord had bit in hard all day long. It took Slocum a few seconds more to free the man's other hand.

After that, the other two stakes came free quickly. The Indian sat up, rubbed his wrists and ankles, then struggled with the cord across his mouth. He gasped in relief when he got the knot untied.

"Come on," Slocum said. "We can get the woman and—"

"They kill me if I stay," the Indian said, scuttling away toward the safety of the dark forest. Slocum grabbed for him, but his hands slid off the man's filthy skin. Looking over his shoulder, Slocum saw that the five in the camp were still sleeping. But how could he spirit Faith away without help from the now-freed, shifty Indian?

Slocum realized he had made a mistake freeing the Indian first. If the guard awoke and saw the prisoner gone, the hue and cry would go up. Better to have released Faith, though Slocum recognized the problem with that course too. If he had gone after the woman first, the bound Indian might have kicked up a ruckus, thinking to gain favor from his captors. Slocum would have had to kill him then.

On his belly, Slocum made his way closer to Faith Gaynor. She heard him and turned frightened eyes to him.

He put his finger to his lips, cautioning her to silence. Slocum wished he had a knife because his fingers felt clumsy on the small, tight knots used to secure the woman. Only a few feet away slept the Indian Slocum thought to be the leader of the band of warriors. Traces

of war paint remained on his cheeks and forehead, showing he had been on the warpath recently. Slocum imag-
ined the man to be one of those attacking the train. If
he was willing to kidnap the daughter of the lumber
company's superintendent, shooting up a train was nothing.

"Ummm, ummm," moaned Faith.

"Quiet," Slocum cautioned. "He's not sleeping too
soundly."

The Indian rolled over, one shoulder coming out from
under the blanket keeping him warm. Slocum worked
faster and got Faith's hands free. She sagged in relief,
able to rub circulation back into her wrists, no longer
bent double. Slocum worked diligently on the cord
around her neck and freed her.

"Come on. Quiet. Our lives depend on it," he told her.

She clung to him for a moment. Tears ran down her
cheeks and left dusty, muddy tracks, but she did not
make a noise that might betray them. He took her hand
and pulled her gently in the direction taken by the other
fleeing captive.

"Daniel, where's Daniel?" she asked.

"Who's that? The Indian?"

"Yes, I saw him being chased. He comes by the camp
often for handouts, and I know him to be a decent
enough fellow. I wanted to help him."

"What's he done to get five of them on his trail?"

"I don't know. The Pomo don't let outsiders know
much about their affairs."

"He's a Pomo?"

"So are they," Faith said, looking back at the sleeping
Indians.

Slocum could get it all straight later. Daniel might
have done nothing more than cheat his comrades in a
game of chance. He had the look of a sharp character,

one inclined to take the easy way out of any jam. The way Daniel had hightailed it rather than saving the woman who had already risked her life for him told Slocum a great deal about the forest fugitive.

"Do you know where the camp is?"

"The lumbering camp? Why, yes, of course," Faith said, startled. "Don't you?"

"I got turned around following you," Slocum said lamely, not wanting to admit his fever had disoriented him and left him in a pickle. In time he could make his way back, but not knowing precisely where to find Spence and the others had entered into his decision to track Faith's captors and free her.

"We're only a mile from camp," she said. "Uphill and then east along the ridge and you'll find the railroad tracks. It's simple to find the camp from there."

"Good," Slocum said.

"John, you're burning up with fever," Faith said, putting her cool hand on his forehead.

"We've got bigger problems," he told her.

"Daniel ought to have helped you. That rascal can be so slothful!"

Slocum put his arm around Faith, but not to support himself. He clamped his hand over her mouth to quiet her.

The sound of footsteps behind was obvious. Slocum whirled around and found himself fighting the leader of the Pomo.

Strong arms clamped around Slocum and threw him backward. The two men tumbled to the ground, rolling over and over. Slocum was hampered by his injured leg, but still managed to come out on top of the heap. His fingers clamped firmly around the Pomo's windpipe. The tendons stood out on Slocum's forearms as he tightened his grip. He dared not let the man cry out and warn the others in the camp.

If he could kill the Pomo quietly enough, there was a chance he and Faith could get away. A chance. A slim chance.

With a grunt and surge of power, the Pomo threw Slocum off. Slocum crashed to the ground and felt the wind gust out of his lungs. Gasping painfully, he struggled to breathe. Then he realized he faced a man holding a knife.

"You will die," the Pomo promised just before he lunged.

Slocum's hands grabbed the Indian's right wrist. He twisted hard and tried to force the Pomo to drop the deadly sharp knife. His strength wasn't up to the task. He missed being gutted by a fraction of an inch when the Indian thrust the knife, pushing Slocum back awkwardly off balance and getting ready for a second try at driving the thick blade all the way into his enemy's gut.

The sharp report of a gunshot startled Slocum, but not enough to keep him from moving fast when he saw it distracted his opponent even more. He got a grip on the Indian's brawny wrist. This time he succeeded in turning the blade back toward its wielder. The hot rush of blood over Slocum's hand told him he had killed the Pomo.

Slocum looked up to see Faith holding his six-shooter. He had not realized he had dropped it.

"I shot him," she said. "I shot him in the back." She shook her head in disbelief. "I've never killed anyone before."

Slocum looked down at the corpse, but didn't see a bullet hole in the man's back. Taking the pistol from Faith's trembling fingers, he said, "You missed him. But it distracted him enough to give me the advantage I needed."

His bloody hand grabbing hers, he pulled the woman toward the shelter of the dark forest a few yards distant. If luck courted them, they could get into the forest before the four remaining Pomo Indians figured out what was going on.

Slocum had experienced a long run of bad luck. It was time for it to change.

But it didn't. Whooping and hollering like devils from hell, the four Indians ran straight for them.

6

Slocum pushed Faith behind him, lifted his Colt Navy, and squeezed off a shot. It missed the leading Indian. Worse, it caused the four Indians to scatter, making it harder for Slocum to miss one and hit another by accident. He shot twice more, this time winging one of the Pomo coming after them.

"Into the woods," Slocum said. "Head for camp. We need to get some help." He fired until his six-shooter was empty, then ran after the red-haired woman. His leg twinged badly, but Slocum wasn't paying any attention to it. If he did, he would die—and he'd take Faith along with him to hell.

They had left the Pomo war party leader dead. That act alone would infuriate the other Indians, but Slocum reckoned something more drove them. Why were they attacking the lumbering camp and shooting up the California Western Railroad in the first place? Whatever riled them, Slocum and Faith were only the latest thorns in their sides.

He crashed through the undergrowth and joined Faith on a game trail. She stood on the path, looking confused.

"The camp," he said, panting hard. "Run for it."

"John, I don't know which direction." She turned left

and then right, seeking some landmark. The tall red-woods masked the sky and made everything look the same no matter which direction she looked. To complicate the matter, fog crept through the trees, giving the woods an eerie sameness in all directions.

"What are we going to do, John? If we run in the wrong direction, we'll head away from camp."

"What's the difference?" Slocum asked, grabbing her hand and pulling her along. He headed in a direction he thought was uphill. Then as the fog shrouded them, Slocum stopped and canted his head to one side, listening hard. The fog dampened sound as much as it deposited water droplets on his face, but Slocum heard movement behind them. He motioned Faith to silence, then got off the trail, heading into the woods.

They blundered fifty yards before Slocum stopped. A huge stump showed that the lumberjacks had worked there recently. He sank down, letting the ten-foot-high stump protect his back. Slocum worked to reload his six-gun.

"What are we going to do?" moaned Faith. "I don't know where we are."

"The stump says we're not far away from camp," Slocum said. "If we sit tight, the Pomo might give up and hightail it."

"Why'd they kidnap me?" she asked, sitting beside him. He laid the six-shooter across his knees, trying to make out approaching Indians in the ever-shifting, form-less fog. Slocum realized he was creating phantasms where none existed. He blinked away the ghosts, waiting for flesh-and-blood Pomo to show themselves before he fired.

Next to him Faith snuggled closer and took his arm. She laid her head on his shoulder. He felt her sobs as hot tears soaked into his shirt.

"It'll be all right," he promised her. "I'll get you back to your pa."

"Thank you for lying to me, John. I know how desperate our situation is. And it's all my fault. If I hadn't tried to save Daniel, they wouldn't have kidnapped me and you wouldn't have had to save me and—"

"Hush," Slocum said.

"Do you hear them coming?" Fright caused the lovely redhead to stiffen and grip his arm even harder.

"No, you're working yourself into a lather for no reason. What do you really know about Daniel?"

Faith shrugged. "Not much. He begs for handouts. He does some odd jobs, but other than that, he's just another Indian."

"Might be he saw something the others wanted to keep him from telling Spence or your pa." Slocum's mind turned over all the details he knew. Daniel was friendly enough with those running the lumbering camp. He might have learned something about the attacks on the Fort Bragg Lumber Company supplies and personnel. If so, the other Indians would want to silence him for being a traitor.

"Could be," she said, "but Daniel never seemed too alert, if you know what I mean. I think he drinks heavily when he can get the firewater."

Slocum knew they could endlessly gnaw on this piece of tough meat and never come to a good conclusion. He changed the subject. "What were you doing out in the forest? Looking for Daniel?"

"Oh, no. Li wanted some herbs, and I promised to get them for him. Don't tell my father. He tolerates the Chinese and doesn't want me consorting with them. And Spence gets upset if I even talk to them."

"I noticed Spence didn't cotton much to the Celestials." Slocum also guessed that the reason there were so many of the Chinese in camp was owing to their willingness to work hard for next to no pay. The lumber company might go out of business if it tried to pay a fair wage for the labor put in by the handful of Chinamen.

"Spence doesn't much like anyone," Faith said somewhat bitterly. Slocum read a great deal into her words, as if she was disappointed with the man. It sounded more like a woman facing the failures of her man than someone analyzing the shortcomings of an employee.

"How long are we going to just sit and do nothing, John?" she asked. "I'm getting spooked. I never liked the fog, but I see things moving when there's nothing there."

Slocum did not respond. He had pushed past that. Or had he?

He pressed a finger against the woman's red lips, then pointed into the fog. The swirling movement was something more than gentle wind blowing through the mist. Someone moved there.

Slocum raised his pistol and aimed carefully. A sudden parting of the fog revealed a Pomo, rifle clutched in his hand. Slocum fired as the Indian spotted them. The bullet caught the Indian high in the chest, spinning him about. Slocum took off at a dead run, stumbling and falling in time to tackle the warrior before he could get back to his feet.

In a heap, the two went down. Slocum ended the fight fast, picking up a short dry stick and using it to strangle the fighting man. When the last death throes ended, Slocum grabbed the fallen rifle and turned to see Faith staring at him, hand to her mouth and her eyes wide.

"We can't stay here," Slocum said. "The others are bound to be near."

"You killed him," she said in a tiny voice.

"I had to," Slocum said.

"I know." She looked at him, even more horror in her eyes. "You had to—and I *wanted* to! He said terrible things to me, even more than their leader. If I'd had the chance, I would have killed him with my bare hands!"

Slocum said nothing. Faith had to come to grips with her own need to survive and what she would do to accomplish it. Some city folks never got used to the sudden death on the frontier, even when it smacked them in the face. He was glad to see that Faith was coming around to realize what it meant to kill a man. And that it was sometimes necessary.

Through the fog they blundered, eventually finding an overhang on the side of the hill that afforded some protection. Slocum and Faith collapsed on a bed of dried leaves and pine needles. He rested a few minutes, his leg throbbing. Then he worked to pull bushes and a few tree limbs with foliage still bushy and green up to conceal their hidey-hole.

He sank back, his entire body aching.

"Are you feverish again?" she asked, putting her hand on his cool forehead.

"Don't think so," Slocum said. When Faith went to remove her hand, he caught her by the wrist and held her. "I like your touch."

"Do you now?" she said, a smile curling the corners of her lips. She ran her fingers down his cheek, across the stubble of his chin, and to his lips. Her fingers lightly worked back and forth. Then she lowered her face and replaced her fingers with her own lips.

The kiss was deep and passionate. Slocum found himself anticipating what would come next. He was not disappointed when Faith sat up suddenly, stared at him with an unfathomable expression, then began unbuttoning her blouse. Her breasts tumbled out, firm and round and ex-

citing. The snowy white cones of flesh were capped with
cherry-bright nipples. The combination of the cool forest
air and her growing excitement visibly hardened the tiny
caps of rubbery nubbins.

Slocum pushed himself up to one elbow and buried
his face between those sweet breasts. He licked and
kissed and then worked a wet spiral up the left breast to
the top. His eager tongue captured the pulsating nub so
he could suck the tip into his mouth.

"Oh, John, yes, so nice. I . . . I feel so strange inside.
So good!"

He continued to minister to her breasts, lavishing
them with kisses until she was gasping for breath. Faith
sank back flat on the ground, her eyes half closed.

"More, John. Give me more."

"What else do you want?" he teased. It was his turn
to gasp when she boldly grasped his crotch and
squeezed. His hardness could not be denied. Faith
reached down with her other hand and hastily pulled
open the buttoned fly. Slocum's manhood snapped out,
firm and round and throbbingly alive.

"So big," Faith whispered. "You're a stallion!"

"What do you do with a stallion?" he asked, his own
hands moving under her skirt and stroking along the
sleekness of her bare legs, moving upward and spreading
her thighs. He stopped when he came to the bushy forest
nestled between her legs. Her Venus mound was already
damp with need for him.

"You ride him. Ride me, John. Ride me!"

Her slender legs rose on either side of Slocum's body.
He moved to position himself at the vee, but he moved
too slowly for her. Faith reached down and gripped him
firmly, tugging hard until the head of his shaft nudged
into her pinkly scalloped nether lips.

Slocum paused a moment, staring down at the

woman. Her eyes were closed now and her face was
drawn with extreme emotion. Her tongue slipped between her lips, wetting them slightly. Then bright blue
eyes stared up into his green ones.

"Yes, John, yes, yes!"

His hips moved forward. He slowly sank into the
warm, moist Garden of Eden so wantonly offered him.
Inch by inch he moved into her until he was surrounded
by clutching, tight female flesh. Buried balls-deep in her
center, Slocum paused, reveling in the sensations seep-
ing hotly into his loins.

The heat was a slow fuse burning into the powder keg
hidden within his loins. When Faith's muscles tensed
slightly, she squeezed down excitingly on his entire
length. Slocum began to doubt he could stand much
more. He began withdrawing as deliberately as he had
entered this paradise.

"Oh, oh!" she gasped, making tiny sounds deep in her
throat. Faith's eyes closed again. Her head began to toss
from side to side, sending a wild array of hair about her
face in a coppery halo that made her appear more angelic
than human. But it was definitely a wanton woman who
opened herself so eagerly for him. And it was a woman
driven to the limits of desire who hunched up and
ground herself into his groin.

Slocum began moving faster now, in and out like the
piston of a railroad locomotive. The friction mounted
along with their mutual passions. He bent and licked and
kissed and suckled at her breasts, then found his lips
engaged with hers when she reached up with both hands,
gripped the sides of his head, and pulled him down.

Mouths locked, loins locked, they struggled erotically
amid the leaves and pungent odors of the redwood forest
until neither could stand the sexual tension. Slocum flew
back and forth in her slippery female tunnel, and Faith

arched up to meet his every inward thrust.

She gasped out her releasing desires a moment before he spilled his seed. Slocum kept up the rhythm of his lusty movement until he began to melt in her humid interior.

He sank to the ground beside her. Faith snuggled closer, her face buried in his chest.

"Thank you, John."

"Reckon we both enjoyed that," he said.

"No, not just . . . that," Faith said. "You rescued me more than once. There's no telling what might have happened to me if you hadn't been there for me."

"Any time," Slocum said, smiling a little.

"I hope so," Faith said, then drifted off to sleep. Slocum held her until dawn, when they made love again.

"There's camp," Faith said in relief. "I was so turned around, I didn't know if I could find it."

Before they had gone a dozen steps both Spence and Faith's father came running up.

"My dear, are you all right?" Ed Gaynor took in his daughter's disheveled condition, then held her in a tight hug. "I've been so worried."

"Yeah," Spence chimed in, "what's been goin' on?" From the hot look he fixed on Slocum, it was apparent he knew—and did not approve. Slocum had wondered, from the way Faith spoke of him, if Spence was sweet on her. The barely suppressed anger Slocum read in Spence's eyes told him it was true.

"Rescued her from some Pomo. Think they were the ones that attacked the train the other day," Slocum said.

"If you got use of that leg back," Spence said, cutting off Slocum's explanation, "git on down to the big tree we been workin' on. We can use all hands on it." He jerked his thumb over his shoulder in the direction of loud sawing sounds.

"Father, you need to let John tell you all he's found. The Pomo—"

"There, there, my dear. Don't get yourself worked up. There will be time later. After you have recovered from your ordeal." To his foreman, Gaynor said, "Be sure there are guards posted. If Slocum's right, the Indians might attack us again."

"The ones that are left," Slocum said, watching Spence's reaction. He failed to decipher what thoughts rattled around in the foreman's head.

Faith and her father went off toward her cabin. Spence squared off in front of Slocum and said, "You might have Gaynor flummoxed, but not me. You're nothing but a malingerer. There's nothin' wrong with your leg, is there?"

Slocum's leg hurt like hell, but he wasn't going to let on to the foreman.

"I can still do a day's work and then some," Slocum said, facing down the foreman.

"Then do it. And you ain't gettin' paid for the time you were off traipisin' around the forest. I don't care what Gaynor says!"

Slocum left the foreman and walked painfully downhill. He saw Li and Chan watching. The Celestials said nothing, and their impassive faces revealed even less about what they thought than Spence's had about his motives.

Rufus spotted Slocum and waved to him from the fifteen-foot-high ledge sawed into a huge sequoia.

"Hey, Slocum, you're jist in time!"

"You mean you need a real man to finish the job?" Slocum shot back. He eyed the rope ladder up to the ledge with some trepidation. Climbing the shaky ladder was hard enough with two good legs. He needed another treatment of Li's poultice, but wasn't about to ask until he had finished his shift. Slocum had the notion that Spence would watch him carefully and use any excuse to fire him.

There might be a knock-down-drag-out fight with Faith in his corner, but Slocum knew how the fight would end. Gaynor would have to choose between a man who had worked for him only a couple days and an experienced logger and foreman.

Somehow, Slocum wasn't ready to drift on. Not yet.

"Hell, no, Slocum. We got a half hour's sawing to do. We kin do that. You in the competition or not?"

"What competition?"

Rufus and the others on the ledge scrambled down, all eager now. Rufus pulled a bright blue ribbon from his pocket. Lou drew out a green one. The others who had been working on the tree showed him a rainbow of colored ribbons.

"We got a pool going. Two dollars and yer in. You take half a ribbon—you got the orange one left, Lou? Good!—and tie it to a stake where you think the tree'll drive it into the ground when it topples."

"So?"

"So whoever's stake is farthest out and is driven all the way into the ground wins the pot. We got forty dollars right now."

"That's a mighty handsome reward for guessing," Slocum said.

"Not guessing, not the way a real lumberjack does it!" boasted Lou. The others on the tree gathered round, waiting to see what Slocum's response would be.

"Don't count on that forty dollars in the pot," Slocum

said slowly. "Make it forty-two. And I'm going to take it all!"

"That's the spirit," Rufus said, clapping Slocum on the back. Slocum pulled out two dollars in crumpled greenbacks and handed it to Rufus. Lou gave him the long orange ribbon.

"Put it anywhere you want. Halfway to Fort Bragg's good 'cuz that'll mean we stand a better chance of winning," joked Rufus.

"Hey, everyone," bellowed another of the loggers from uphill. "Mr. Gaynor wants to talk to us. Spence says to knock off and get your butts up here right away."

"Go on, Slocum," Rufus said. "Plant your stake jist like the rest of ours. Leave a foot or so out of the ground, though it don't matter much. If the tree hits it, that's a couple tons of wood mallet drivin' it into the ground."

"Spence says to move it right *now!*"

Slocum took the orange ribbon and watched the others trudging uphill toward the camp. He eyed the tree, saw where the deep vee cut had been made, and estimated the redwood's height. Then he began walking, looking over his shoulder now and then to peer through the branches of other trees at the tip of the giant sequoia. He stopped, and was heartened to see a half-dozen stakes with varicolored ribbons around. He wasn't the only one guessing this to be the spot where the tree would fall.

But he thought the tree was shorter than the others. He moved back a few yards, got a decent stake, and started driving it into the soft humus until it poked up about a foot. As he tied the orange ribbon on, he heard a gunshot.

Or he thought it was a gunshot at first. Slocum looked up and saw the mighty redwood toppling over straight for him.

7

Slocum froze in place, staring as the giant sequoia fell with agonizing slowness toward him. With a burst of understanding about what was happening, Slocum spun and dug in his toes, trying to run, to accelerate enough to avoid certain death if the hundred-ton tree landed on him. He struggled to run, but his feet slipped on the leaf-strewn slick forest floor.

Falling full-length, Slocum rolled and put his arms up over his head to protect his neck as he lay facedown in a narrow gully running downhill in the direction of the falling tree.

The impact of the redwood hitting the ground knocked the wind out of him. He felt sharp pain the entire length of his body. Then a curious nothingness followed. Slocum seemed to float in space, tumbling endlessly, not breathing, not living, not dying. But the pain convinced him he was still alive. He could not believe death would bring such eternal pain with it.

Unless he had died and gone to hell.

In the distance came frightened, excited voices. New thumping on the ground communicated to him as he pressed his ear to the forest floor. Slocum tried to stand, but could not move his body. Struggling now, he attempted to free his arms, but they were pinned in place above his head. Wiggling from side to side got him nowhere. He was trapped, pinned under the immense weight of the tree.

"Help!" he cried out. Slocum listened. The voices came closer. He shouted again and again until he attracted someone's attention.

"He's alive. Glory be, he's alive but crushed under the tree. Get axes. We kin chop him out! You hang on now, Slocum, and we'll git you out in nothin' flat!"

Slocum recognized Lou's voice. He tried to thank the man, but pressure on his back crushed the air from his lungs and the life from his body. All Slocum could do was hope they hurried. He lay under the tree, taking short, shallow breaths that did nothing to convince him he was going to survive. Then vibration shook him. Every time an ax blow landed on the tree, he felt it the entire length of his body.

Then, like magic, the weight vanished from his body. Hands grabbed at him and pulled him up from what might have been a grave, had the gully been any shallower.

"You're about the dangedest, luckiest jasper I ever seen," Rufus said. "A tree fell on you and you kin walk away from it."

"With your help," Slocum said, brushing himself off. "Thanks. All of you." He looked around. Lou wiped perspiration off his face. He had been using the ax like a madman on the tree limb pinning Slocum to the ground. Others laughed and joked and congratulated one another. Only Spence stood apart, an expression approaching hatred on his face.

"What you all standing around lollygaggin' for?" Spence bellowed. "Get on back to work now."

Lou slapped Slocum on the shoulder and returned to

work. The sequoia had been felled. Now they had to take off the upper limbs and prepare it for the float downriver to Fort Bragg and the sawmill.

"You're a mess, Slocum," Spence said. "Get some decent clothes on. And see if somebody back at the camp can't patch you up some. I don't want you bleedin' like that while you work." Spence glared at him.

"I won't be long," Slocum said. He watched Spence whirl around and bark orders that weren't needed to the crew trimming the tree. The loggers knew their business; Spence only wanted some way to vent his anger.

Slocum didn't go straight back to camp. He detoured past the tall stump where the redwood had stood so proudly only minutes earlier. The first tree had broken because of rotted sections. Slocum remembered that sound well, as well as the sound of the healthy wood snapping. What he had heard this time was more of a gunshot.

"Or explosion," he said, looking at the butt end of the felled sequoia. Burn marks showed where a stick or two of dynamite had blown away the supporting wood and caused the tree to topple. Or were those marks old lightning scars? The tree had endured hundreds of years in the forest. Slocum had no way of telling, until he touched the charred portion.

The soot came off on his hand. The blast was of recent origin. Within a handful of minutes, Slocum guessed.

Hardly satisfied, but feeling a bit surer of his welcome in the lumbering camp, he made his way painfully up the side of the canyon and along the ridge to the camp. His numerous cuts bled and hurt like a son of a gun. Every movement plastered more of his shirt and trousers to the bloody wounds on his back and legs.

Chan and a few other Chinese came out and watched silently as he limped along. As bad as he looked, he felt worse. His bruised leg was acting up too, making every movement a living hell.

"You are hard to kill," observed Li. "Maybe next time they succeed."

"What do you mean?" Slocum dropped to the ground near the Celestials and looked up at them. They stood passively, hands folded and watching him intently, but making no move toward him to help.

Li shrugged. "Accidents are everywhere. Around you, and everywhere. Many men hurt in camp past few months, many leave and never come back. New loggers are no good."

"My luck's been doing poorly of late," Slocum admitted, smiling crookedly at the notion of ever having good luck again. "You have a potion to change it?"

"No," said Li. He held out his hand, and another of the Celestials put a small jar in his hand. "I do have more poultice for your leg. Missy Gaynor get herbs I need. The other damage to your back . . ." Li shrugged again.

"I'd like it if you could fix me up the best you could. There's not a doctor this side of Fort Bragg, and the leg was working pretty good until I banged it up again." Slocum stretched out his right leg. The bruised muscle throbbed again, the recipient of too much new damage to ever heal any time soon.

"I know these things," said Li.

"And Miss Gaynor got you some herbs from the forest," Slocum said. Li fixed dark eyes on him. Slocum thought a hint of a smile crossed the man's lips, but couldn't be certain.

"You go to my tent. I fix you up good."

"I have to get some new clothes," Slocum said. "These are in tatters."

"We fix, we fix," Li assured him. The others scuttled

off, scattering in all directions. Slocum got to his feet, but appreciated the Chinaman's help getting to the tent. The ordeal he'd been through had taken the starch right out of him.

He collapsed on a thin pallet, but started to get off when he realized he was still oozing blood from a dozen cuts on his back. Li pushed him down gently.

"Do not worry about that. Worry about this. It is needful."

Slocum gasped when Li started peeling the shirt off his back. The blood had dried in places, making the removal of the cloth painful. Flesh came along with the shirt, and the wounds bled anew. Slocum lay facedown on the pallet and tried to think of other things. Somehow, no matter how he tried to think about Faith Gaynor or being a thousand miles away, he kept coming back to Spence and the look on the man's face.

It was a look of anger born of failing. Slocum didn't have much money left to bet, but he would put everything on Spence being the one who had tried to kill him. Returning with Faith had been a big mistake, Slocum guessed, making Spence into a jealous monster capable of killing any competition for the woman's affections.

Still, from all Faith had said, she tolerated Spence rather than liking him.

Slocum winced with every strip, and then bit down hard on the edge of the pallet when Li applied a cold paste to the wounds. The soothing coolness turned to white-hot pain in a flash, making Slocum's entire body feel as if it had been thrust into a blast furnace.

"It is good for you," Li assured him. "A little pain now, none later."

"A little?" Slocum closed his eyes and rode out the waves of agony. He had been shot by outlaws and kicked by horses and had bones broken in falls. Even the massive bruise on his thigh had not hurt this much. When the pain reached a point where Slocum thought he would go out of his head, the torment eased. As he relaxed, the pain flowed away faster and faster like the tide rolling back out to sea.

"I do feel better. Thanks, Li."

"You need more of this, Slocum," the Chinese said, handing him a jar of the disgusting-smelling poultice. "*That* is serious wound."

"Thanks. I'll go to my tent and—" Slocum tried to stand, but turned light-headed and had to sit again.

"You wait. We go work, come back, and see how you do. But you rest."

"Thanks," Slocum said, knowing Spence would come hunting him if he didn't get back to work. But the way the world spun in crazy, wild circles all around him prevented standing, much less working. Slocum gingerly smeared the unguent onto his thigh and then rubbed it in. The dull throb began to recede just as the pain in his back had.

Chan brought new clothes for him, placed them respectfully at the foot of the pallet, bowed, and backed from the tent. Slocum wondered how he had come to rate so highly with the Celestials. At the moment the only thing he wanted to do was sleep for a week. He lay back down on his belly, and had begun drifting off when he heard loud voices.

"It's out of the question. I've never heard of such a thing," Ed Gaynor said. Slocum lifted the corner of the tent and saw the lumber company superintendent with a short, stout man dressed in a black broadcloth coat, fancy brocade gold vest, and shoes so highly polished Slocum thought the sun's reflection off the toes might blind him. The man stared up at Gaynor, the set to his lantern jaw showing increasing truculence.

"I am a government agent, sir. You cannot mock me with your claims of ignorance!"

"Mr. Elliot, I am not mocking you. It is just that this is so sudden. I need time to work something out, contact Mr. Johnson, who is back East at the moment, find—"

"You will cease all lumbering unless these demands are met. I will have a federal marshal out here so fast, you won't have time to clear those silly spectacles of yours!"

Slocum lowered the tent flap as the men walked toward him. He was intent on spying when they stopped a few feet away.

"There must be a treaty made with the Pomo before you can continue logging operations, sir," Elliot said. "Their claims are quite specific and take precedence over your somewhat dubious permission to cut timber on these lands."

"I've never heard any of the Indians say a thing about this being a burial ground. None of my men has found a trace of a cemetery. From what I know, the Pomo are like the Modoc and the Klamath and cremate their dead. How can they have a burial ground if they burn their dead to ashes?"

"That's not my concern. We have received a legitimate complaint about your desecration of burial sites. Either make a treaty with the Pomo or I assure you the government will not long tolerate your illegal activity here!"

Slocum wondered if Elliot spoke in any way but shrill exclamations. From the expression on Gaynor's face, the government agent had hit a sore spot.

"I don't even know if the Pomo *have* a chief. Who should I see?"

"Their chief," Elliot said coldly. "It is entirely your responsibility finding him. In one week, I will return.

Either have the signed treaty with the tribe or be prepared to cease and desist all logging operations. I will then see to removing you from the land, forcibly if needed."

"Can you show me where the graveyard is? I don't get into the forest much, but my foreman does and he hasn't seen any sign of it. He would have told me."

"Mr. Gaynor, good day. You have one week and not an instant longer!" Elliot stalked off, clutching a small leather case to his chest. Slocum dropped the tent flap and forced himself to his feet. Unsteadily making his way out, he almost walked into Gaynor. The man was lost in thought—or worry.

"Mr. Gaynor," Slocum said. "I couldn't help overhearing what that popinjay said."

"Mr. Elliot is a government agent from Fort Bragg. He wants to close us down."

"What's the problem with the Indians?"

"Mr. Elliot claims the Pomo are furious at our desecration of their burial grounds and thus we are responsible for raids on both the town of Willits a few miles to the east and even on Fort Bragg. If he is right, why, we might be inciting the Pomo to attack our supply trains, including the one you rode in on, Slocum."

"Those are mighty big supposes," Slocum said. "Does Elliot have the authority he claims?"

"I believe he might. The federal marshal in Fort Bragg is no friend of C. R. Johnson, no, sir. They locked horns early on when C. R. refused to pay him money for protection. Extortion, it was. But I thought all that had been smoothed out."

"How hard would it be finding the Pomo chief?" Slocum asked. "Get him to sign a treaty you draw up and you can tell Elliot to go whistle in the dark."

"Would that the matter were so easily solved," Gaynor said. "The Pomo are an amorphous bunch. I am not sure they even *have* a chief or the concept of one. It is widely known that there isn't even a single tribe calling themselves Pomo, other than how they all mean it."

"I've heard," Slocum said. He remembered that Pomo meant "the People," and all the tribes could claim to be Pomo using that definition.

"I must find the Pomo chief and negotiate. That sounds so simple, but it is anything but. Mr. Slocum, you are a man of the world. I can tell that you are no common laborer. How would *you* find the Pomo chief?"

At the edge of the camp Slocum saw Daniel sneaking about, stealing food from behind the mess tent.

"I think I might find you the Pomo chief," Slocum said slowly. "When I do, I'll bring him straightaway to you."

"Thank you, thank you," Gaynor said absently. "I'll be in my cabin. So much work to do, and if Mr. Elliot closes down the camp, why, how will we ever supply the wood we contracted for with the sawmill?" The man walked away, muttering to himself.

Slocum judged the direction Daniel took after he'd grabbed handfuls of food, then cut through the forest and came out on a trail ahead of the scrawny Indian.

Daniel recoiled and dropped the food when Slocum seemed simply to appear in front of him on the game trail.

"You!" cried the Pomo, eyes wide with astonishment. "You are alive."

"No thanks to you. I saved your worthless hide. You should have stayed and helped me save Miss Gaynor."

"She is dead?"

"She's alive, as if you cared," snapped Slocum.

"Then you did not need me, so there is no reason to be angry with me."

The argument struck Slocum as ridiculous. Then he had to laugh.

"All right, but you owe Miss Gaynor a favor. A big one."

"I'll clean her cabin. I've done that before."

"And I'll bet valuable items vanished along with you," Slocum said, reaching out and grabbing the Indian's shirt. He shook, and silverware, along with odds and ends from around camp, tumbled to the ground. Daniel dropped to his knees and scooped them back up.

"Just taking these to clean. My treat."

"Daniel, you're going to do more than this for Miss Gaynor." Slocum grabbed the Indian's thin arm and pulled him to his feet. Daniel was hardly five feet tall and didn't look as if he had eaten a square meal in months. From the way he ran, though, Slocum knew he was lithe and had a wiry strength lurking in the bony body.

"What do you want?"

"Who's your chief? Who's chief of the Pomo? Can you take me to him?"

"Chief? Of the Pomo? We don't have a chief. Too many small bands, each with its own leader. A bad hunt and the leader changes. A good hunt and maybe he stick around for another hunt."

Slocum had seen this structure often in nomadic Indians. No single man claimed the right as chief. The Apache voted on war chiefs, and might change their leader with every raid.

"You can't point to any Pomo and say he's your leader?"

Daniel shook his head. A slow smile curled Slocum's lips.

"Come on. We're going to see Mr. Gaynor."

"Wait, I have done nothing wrong. You can't have

me whipped again. Don't let Spence whip me again!"

"Spence wouldn't dare whip the chief of the Pomo tribe, now would he?" Slocum asked.

Daniel looked confused. Then realization of what Slocum meant dawned on him. He drew himself up to his full five-foot height and positively strutted into the logging camp. One instant he had been a garbage-stealing thief. The next he was Chief Daniel of the Pomo Nation.

Slocum hoped Elliot would be as easily convinced.

8

"No, sir, never thought he was the chief kind," Rufus said, staring curiously at the new Pomo chief. Daniel strutted around the camp, ordering people around. Mostly, they obeyed, amused that the scrawny scavenger had enough sand to order them to do anything. Slocum knew that would wear off eventually, but all that mattered was the government agent believing that Daniel *was* a chief and could sign treaties for his tribe.

"Just goes to show, you can't judge a book by its cover," Slocum said, trying not to laugh. He stretched, and felt a few twinges along his back where the redwood limbs had cut him. Li's salve had fixed him right up. Even his thigh felt better. Not back to normal, but good enough for him to do a day's work and not worry about his body giving way under him.

"Get your butts to work," bellowed Spence. "I'm not payin' you to stand around jawin' all day." The foreman went through camp, his face red from the strain of yelling at his crew.

"Got a bug up his ass, he does," Rufus observed. "He's always been a high-strung one, but of late he's gettin' on my nerves." As if to emphasize the point, Rufus took a flask out of his big hip pocket and knocked back a quick swig.

Slocum watched the bowler-wearing, dapper foreman make his rounds as he rousted one after another of the lumbering crew. When Spence came to Chief Daniel, he stared at the Indian with a belligerent set to his jaw, as if he was going to call out the impostor. Slocum didn't know if Ed Gaynor had let the foreman in on the deception. From the way Spence glared at the Pomo, Slocum doubted it. Keeping the charade a secret seemed a good idea, even if Spence had every reason to do all he could to keep the logging operation going.

Or did he?

"You're no chief," Spence raged thrusting his face close to Daniel's. To Slocum's surprise, the Indian didn't back down. With a quiet dignity, Daniel tossed his tattered blanket over one shoulder like some ancient Roman senator and looked down his long, straight nose at the foreman.

"You are no foreman," Daniel said haughtily. "Which is true? Which is a lie?"

"You—" Spence cocked back his fist, ready to unload a punch that would knock out the Indian. Lou came up and grabbed his boss's hand.

"Don't go doin' anything that'll rile them savages more," Lou said. "You know what happened last night."

Spence relaxed, took a deep breath, and stalked off. Lou followed. Slocum turned to Rufus, wondering at Lou's comment.

"What happened?" Slocum asked. "I haven't heard anything."

Rufus made a wry face. "More trouble. Trouble done by them heathens. If Daniel's a chief, we ought to hold him responsible for what all his people do."

"Trouble? More trouble on the railroad?"

"You ask a lot of questions, Slocum," Rufus said. He stomped off, following others down the trail to the new sequoia they had begun working on the day before.

Slocum frowned. Folks were getting real nervy in the camp. Rufus was a good man, as was Lou, but both were ready to tear the head off anyone making simple conversation. From all Slocum could tell, the number of lumberjacks in the camp had decreased substantially over the past month. That explained Spence's eagerness to recruit anyone the least bit interested in the job. No trees being cut meant no money for the Fort Bragg Lumber Company, and no money put them out of business fast.

Making his way through the tents, Slocum stopped in the "Chinese village," as he had come to think of it. The tents were set away from the others, as if the Celestials might bring the plague with them. Slocum stared at Chan, whose bruised and cut face looked like a side of freshly cut beef.

"What happened to you?" Slocum asked. Chan bowed without saying a word and hurried off. Slocum found the same reluctance to speak among the other Chinamen too. He finally backed Li against a tree so he couldn't go scuttling off.

"I know nothing," Li said sullenly.

"Chan's face looks like he was worked over good. Who did it?" Slocum had the feeling he knew the answer. "Did Spence do it?" Li still did not answer, but Slocum read the truth in the Celestial's face.

"We permit damage to the camp food," Li finally said. "Punishment was just."

"The hell it was," Slocum said coldly. "Somebody sneaked into camp last night and destroyed our supplies. Is that what happened?"

Li nodded once, then feinted to the right and moved left, easily avoiding Slocum. He let the Chinaman go. He had work to do, and so did Li. But everyone thought the Pomo had done the damage. Why beat up Chan, unless it was to vent frustration?

Slocum had seen the cruel edge to the foreman's character. He vowed to watch Spence more carefully, especially considering the incident with the tree. Slocum had no proof Spence had dynamited the trunk to cause the tree to fall, but that seemed the way to bet.

Working hard all day, Slocum and Rufus sawed one notch after another in the side of the three-hundred-foot sequoia, moving the boards they stood on ever higher until they were close to twenty feet above the ground.

"This is where we get down to real work," Rufus said, spitting on his callused hands and grabbing the axes being handed up to them. "You up for some hard work, Slocum?" He tossed an ax to Slocum, then began with a steady chopping on the iron-hard trunk of the towering redwood.

Slocum fell into a steady rhythm with Rufus, one chopping while the other drew back for the next stroke. How long he worked Slocum could not say, but a pile of chips grew ankle-deep around both men. When they took a break, Lou came up and brushed the chips off to ensure a secure footing on the plank ledge. Then they went back to work. After long hours of backbreaking chopping, Slocum was dog-tired and there seemed to be little to show for their efforts.

"It's not two feet into the trunk," he said, shaking his head.

"Good work, Slocum," Rufus said. "This tree's goin' faster than the last three or four, thanks to you. You're the first one to get hired in a month who can keep up with me."

"Fast?" Slocum could hardly believe it. "We're going slow!"

Rufus chuckled, took a sip of his whiskey, and passed

it over to Slocum, who drank sparingly of the potent firewater.

"Felling trees has slowed down a lot in the past few weeks," Rufus said. "That's makin' the boss jittery as a mouse in a cat factory. At this rate, we'll have this tree down by the end of the week."

"What then?" Slocum asked.

Rufus shrugged. "We find another one and start all over. There's trees aplenty in the forest. Just a matter of work gettin' 'em chopped down."

At the end of the day, Slocum plodded back to camp, his shoulders aching more than his leg. He was used to hard work, but cutting down the redwoods was *hard* work. As he made his way to his tent, he saw Faith Gaynor in the door of her cabin. She motioned to him to join her. Slocum was loath to do that, not wanting to start rumors—and not wanting to cross Spence.

But her insistent gestures would create more of a fuss than them being seen together. Slocum went over and said, "Evening, Miss Gaynor."

"John, I need to speak to you. In private!"

"Wouldn't look right," Slocum said, aware of the other lumberjacks making their way slowly back to camp in time for chuck. Rumors flew around camp faster than at any women's sewing circle. The men were miles from the nearest recreation and had nothing better to do.

"My father's office," Faith said. "That's neutral territory." She hurried over, Slocum trailing behind. Even from the rear Slocum found her a beguiling woman. He enjoyed the way her bustle-sporting rump bounced about, and even caught sight of an ankle as she lifted her skirts to go up the steps to her father's office. Slocum followed her inside, but did not close the door. This might be better than getting together in her cabin, but they were still liable to cause tongues to wag.

"John, I don't know how to say this," Faith began. She looked flustered, distraught. Spots of red in her cheeks showed how agitated she was. Slocum knew it had to be the raid made on the camp the prior night upsetting her.

"Any idea who got into the food supplies?" he asked bluntly, cutting through her fog of confusion.

"Why, that *is* what I wanted to speak to you about. How'd you know? Never mind," she said, answering her own question. "Of course, everyone is talking about it. If the food had been stolen, that would have been reasonable, but it was ruined. Kerosene was poured over most of it, making it entirely inedible."

"Heard the Pomo had taken it," Slocum said.

"No, no, it was *ruined*, as if eating it didn't matter to anyone. I've seen the Indians around the camp. If they had found the food, they would have taken it for themselves."

"So," said Slocum, "the destroyed supplies were left as a warning?"

"I had not thought of that, but it might be true," Faith said. "Something has to be done, John. The company cannot survive long without cash coming in for a half-dozen more logs. Mr. Johnson has authorized my father to do whatever is necessary, but—"

"But your pa can't figure out what's necessary," Slocum finished. He didn't know Ed Gaynor well, but saw the man might be better suited to adding up columns of numbers than running the lumbering company on a day-to-day basis. Gaynor left that chore to Spence, and Spence was spending more time snapping and snarling like a rabid dog than getting work done.

"We need your help, John." Faith looked straight at him with her wide, bright blue eyes. She might have been an angel come to earth. She added in a husky whisper, "*I* need your help."

"I'll see what can be done," Slocum promised. He was rewarded by a quick, fleeting kiss. Then Faith left. Slocum followed quickly, stopped just outside the office, and looked around to see if anyone had noticed them being together alone. Most of the loggers were busy eating. Only the Chinese, huddled over their single bowls of rice, might have noticed. Slocum doubted any of them had much truck with the white men in camp. He walked slowly to the mess tent and sat at the end of a long table, looking around at the men avidly eating anything put in front of them. Slocum did a quick head count and saw there were two fewer at the table than before.

The company continued to lose men, as well as supplies.

Slocum finished and left hurriedly, not partaking of the give-and-take joking. The men would soon enough get back to work, sharpening saws and ax blades, preparing for tomorrow's chopping.

The cool night air carried the heavy scents of a forest. Redwood and spruce, some pine, and the lush undergrowth all mingled to cause Slocum's nostrils to flare. This was quite a place, serene and quiet.

Movement at the edge of camp caught Slocum's sharp eye. He drifted like a ghost, then walked faster to get close to the spot where someone had been lurking. Slocum dropped to one knee and made out the boot print in the soft ground. He couldn't be positive, but thought this was Spence's track. The darkness made tracking difficult, although Spence made no effort to hide his tracks.

Slocum picked up the pace, going along a game trail, seeing this was the direction Spence was heading in away from camp. Slocum ran the risk of overtaking the foreman in the dark, but felt the necessity for speed outweighed caution. Why, Slocum couldn't say, but Spence's actions seemed suspicious.

Slocum would have taken the vague assignment of finding out what was going on at the logging camp just for Faith, but after the redwood had almost crushed him to death, he felt a personal stake in finding out what was going on. He wanted to be certain Spence was the one responsible before he took him out.

Slocum had to admit there might be more to the troubles than met the eye. He wanted to know everything. Why putting the Fort Bragg Lumber Company out of business was important to anyone baffled him. There wasn't anything special about this patch of sequoia forest that a competitor couldn't find somewhere a mile north or south. For all that, Slocum wasn't sure who the competition for the company might be. Neither Ed Gaynor nor his daughter had mentioned rivals in the business. Considering the dearth of lumber in San Francisco, a dozen companies ought to be able to sell all they could cut and never have to worry about interfering with each other.

Slocum walked along, slowing now when he saw that Spence's footprints were not as widely spaced, showing the foreman was slowing his headlong pace into the forest. With half a mind on the trail, Slocum thought about other possible reasons for the troubles in camp. Maybe Ed Gaynor had ruffled somebody's feathers. Or C. R. Johnson. The owner of the company spent a powerful lot of time back East raising money. He might have angered some banker in San Francisco or New York or elsewhere.

That made no sense, though. A banker wanted money, not revenge. Slocum had never met a banker who didn't think in terms of profits over any personal vendetta. And the Pomo Indians added another puzzle that muddied the water.

From all accounts, the Pomo were a scattered group without a strong sense of tribe. Even calling any one tribe Pomo was wrong, no matter what the locals said. Being in an uproar over a violated burial ground didn't jibe with what Slocum had seen of the Indians calling themselves Pomo. The one band had been moving inland, heading toward their sacred mountain of Shasta. And the other group, the one kidnapping Daniel and Faith, had seemed to be operating on their own.

None of it made any sense. Yet.

Voices slipped through the trees and warned Slocum that Spence and at least one other man were ahead. He left the game trail and quietly made his way through the thick brush to a spot where he could peer from behind a spruce tree into a half-moon-shaped clearing. Starlight provided only faint illumination, but Slocum recognized the two men right away. Somehow, he wasn't too surprised.

"You were supposed to *take* it, you fool!" raged Spence. "We needed it."

"Don't go calling me a fool," Elliot, the government agent, said angrily. "There wasn't time. We almost got caught. How'd that look?"

"But you *spoiled* it!"

"We can get more."

"We have to pay for it out of our own pockets," Spence said glumly. "This was for the taking."

"If you moved faster, it wouldn't be necessary."

"Me? Look who's talking. What are you going to do about Gaynor finding that Pomo chief? You know how them savages are. Flash a few trinkets in front of 'em, and they'll agree to anything. If Daniel signs a treaty, what are you goin' to do then?"

"This is a joke," Elliot said. "Daniel's no chief. Hell, there's not even a Pomo tribe! How can he be chief of a tribe that doesn't even exist? This is something Gaynor thought up to stymie us."

"He's not that smart," Spence declared.

"His daughter thought it up then," said Elliot. "She's as smart as she is good-looking."

"Leave Faith out of this," Spence said, his voice turning nasty.

"You got a letch for her, don't you?" Elliot taunted. "Don't think with your balls this time. You can have her after we're done."

Slocum wondered what the two men were talking about. He reckoned Elliot was responsible for destroying the camp food supply. Spence had wanted him to steal it, but something had gone wrong and Elliot had either improvised or panicked and just poured kerosene over it.

But the rest? Slocum couldn't tell.

He drifted from tree to tree, working his way closer to where the men stood at the edge of the clearing. He wasn't sure what this would accomplish, but he wanted to hear everything they said, especially now that their initial anger at one another was dying down and they were lowering their voices.

Slocum got to a spot behind a waist-high stump not ten yards from the men. The government agent went on and on about getting the federal marshal out, the cavalry, seeing if the entire U.S. Army could be involved. As sure as Elliot was that this was a good idea, Spence was opposed. Slocum wanted to know why—and what the pair was conspiring to do.

He had poked his head around the stump to get a better look when they fell silent for several seconds. From the corner of his eye Slocum saw a shadow fashioned by starlight behind a bulky body moving near him. Before he could turn, a heavy branch crashed down onto the top of his head. Slocum slumped against the stump, grabbed it, and then let it go as his arms turned limp. He fell to the ground, unconscious.

9

Slocum groaned and tried to move. He heard distant voices, arguing, shouting, saying things that were important to him if he could only understand.

"I . . ." he muttered. A heavy thud sounded and sent pain arrowing into his shoulder.

"Damn, missed," said a voice he almost recognized. The next blow landed squarely on the top of Slocum's head, again putting him out like a light.

Water splashing on his face woke Slocum from his stupor. He opened his mouth to cry out, to protest this sorry treatment—and was rewarded with a mouthful of choking water. He sputtered and spat and tried to see what was going on.

Water burned his eyes. He couldn't breathe. And his arms and legs felt like lead weights. Worst of all was the cold crushing him from all directions at once.

He shook his head and sent water flying when air again returned to his face. Gasping for breath, Slocum looked straight up and saw only blue sky. Then a rolling sensation carried him to one side and trees flashed by. From the corner of his eyes he saw water approaching like a tidal wave. He sucked in as much air as he could and held his breath as he spun into the creek. This time he kept his eyes open, and saw the riverbed flash past before again emerging into the air.

Slocum spat water and panted, his lungs on fire. He struggled to get free of the ropes tying his arms and legs, but the water was already causing the hemp rope to tighten even more. His hands were freezing lumps of flesh and his legs were gone, long past throbbing with intense pain. He had no idea how long he had been tied like this.

Or where.

He wasn't thinking too clearly until he again swung to the side and was dunked in the creek. As he remained underwater, all the details flooded into his numbed brain. Someone had tied him to the redwood log rolled downhill to Pudding Creek. He was on the log and floating downriver toward Fort Bragg.

"Help!" he yelled when he rolled out of the water. As he struggled harder, the log began rolling faster. Slocum fought to keep air in his lungs as he was again tortured with being held under the surface. Slocum tried to remain calm and still, though little he did affected the massive redwood log.

The irony of the situation was not lost on Slocum. This was the same tree that had almost crushed him flat. It had taken long hours of work chopping off the limbs and readying it for transport down Pudding Creek to the Fort Bragg sawmill. He had no idea when it had been launched or by whom.

If he knew who had kicked the massive sequoia into the river, he would also know who had tied him up to drown. The government man, Elliot, and Spence had to know what was going on, but someone had slugged him while he spied on the two men. He recalled coming to soon after he had been hit and recognizing—almost—the voice of the man responsible.

Then Slocum forgot all about assigning blame and fought to stay alive. The turbulent river kicked the log from side to side and sent it spinning as it traversed the curves on its way to the ocean.

Slocum knew wolves would gnaw off their own legs to get out of a trap. He wished he had the chance. The perpetual torture he endured of being dunked and then, usually too briefly, given the chance to gasp for air tired him quickly. He tried to judge how far down the river he had gone by the speed of the passing limbs overhead. He tried and he failed. Any hope of surviving the trip and being rescued by a sawmill employee faded as Slocum's strength ran out.

Around and around he was spun until he kept his eyes clamped tightly shut. Doggedly hanging on to life, he refused to give up. He had a score to settle with Spence and Elliot. He had a powerful big score to settle with a lot of folks.

But he weakened, even if his determination to live did not. The ropes were too tight and the water too cold. Lungs about to burst, Slocum spun around for what he thought might be his last rotation on the huge redwood log.

Scraping sounds came. Then pain in his right hand as the rope gave way and allowed circulation back. Slocum fought to open his eyes. Water blurred his vision but he saw a small, wet, mostly naked figure sawing away at his left hand. Those ropes parted too, and he was able to reach out to clutch a stub of a limb.

"Get you free quick-like," came the promise. Slocum fought to sit up and see who cut frantically at the ropes holding his ankles. The rope parted suddenly flinging Slocum off the log and into the raging, turbulent water.

He sputtered and flailed and fought, driving hard to reach the surface. He wasn't bound this time, but his

stamina was long gone. Lungs filled with fire, he succeeded in bobbing to the surface of the creek one last
time.

More dead than alive, he tried to float on his back.
Strong hands gripped him and pulled. He tried to help,
but his rescuer ordered him to stop. Slocum realized he
was only hindering his own salvation, and went limp. In
no time, he felt the smooth rocks and cool mud of a
riverbank under him. He lay flat on his back, staring at
the brilliant cobalt-blue sky filled with gathering storm
clouds. That was about the way he felt. At peace—for
the moment.

When he recovered, someone would pay for this.

"You all right?" came the worried question.

Slocum propped himself up on one elbow. His eyes
widened in surprise when he saw his rescuer.

"Chief Daniel," Slocum said. "You surely did pull my
fat out of the fire."

"No, no, I pull you out of river. You would drown if
you stayed much longer." The short Pomo sat cross-
legged on the bank, staring at Slocum. "How did you
get on log? That is dangerous. The logs bang all around
as they go to the ocean."

"When I find out who tied me there," Slocum said,
"someone's going to have to make a coffin or two to
hold them."

Chief Daniel said nothing, sitting and staring intently
at Slocum.

"How'd you happen to save me? I'm much obliged."

"You make me chief. I owe you," Daniel said, grinning. "I was looking for junk washed up on the shore
when I saw log. You cried out. Once. I think, 'Chief
Daniel, there is man in big trouble.' So I run ahead and
climb out on limb over river. When you wash real fast

under me, I jump real faster." Daniel shrugged, as if saying everything else was easy.

Slocum marveled at the bizarre turn of events. The bogus chief of the Pomo had been scavenging along the creek for anything washed away from the lumber camp and had just happened to spot him.

"You're the best choice for chief," Slocum assured him. "You ought to do better than scavenging for dross along the riverbanks. I'll talk to Mr. Gaynor about it and see what can be done."

If Slocum had any money, he would have bought Chief Daniel a new blanket and all the food he could pack away into his scrawny body. For all that, the skinny Indian had shown real courage and more than a little vitality during the rescue. He had kept his head and acted in time to save Slocum from a watery death.

"Did you happen to see who launched the log?" Slocum asked.

Daniel shrugged and shook his head. "I was downriver from where they send logs into water. I did not see who tied you down to die."

"Too bad," Slocum said. He lay back, watched the clouds form into thunderheads over the coast, and worried over who had done this to him. He had spied on Spence and Elliot, but he didn't know for sure if they had had a hand in it. Whoever had slugged him was definitely going to pay for trying to murder him this way. Slocum understood getting shot in a face-to-face gunfight. This was downright cowardly, and they had wanted him to suffer before he died.

The only trouble was, Slocum had no idea who had sneaked up on him so expertly. He suspected Elliot and Spence, but his attacker was certainly responsible for some part of the watery torture. While it was a bad bet, Slocum knew the two conspirators might not even know he had been in the woods spying on them. Slocum might have run afoul of someone else eavesdropping.

"You get me new rifle?" asked Daniel. "I can hunt again. I had good Henry rifle once, but traded it for blanket and food last winter."

"I'll see what can be done," Slocum promised. "Might be I can scare up a Winchester."

Daniel helped him to his feet. Slocum regained strength as he walked, heading back to the logging camp. He wondered who would look shocked when he came walking in with Daniel at his elbow. That would be a giveaway to who had tried to send him down the river to his death.

It was past noon when they entered the camp. Dinner had been served, leaving the Chinese to clean up when the crew went back to logging. Slocum dropped down at the end of a table in the mess tent.

"Got anything left?" he called out to the Chinese cook.

Li came over, looking from Slocum to Daniel and back. "You not eat with others?"

"My friend and I would appreciate some chow," Slocum said. "Anything that's left."

"He eats garbage," Li said, not looking at Daniel. Slocum saw that there was no love lost between the Celestials and the Indians. In this camp everyone had a hatred for everyone else.

"I owe him my life. The least I can do for him is to get him some grub," Slocum said. Li stared at Slocum with unfathomable black eyes, then turned and silently shuffled off. Slocum had no idea if he was going to get fed, if Daniel would be fed too, or if they'd both be tossed out.

He and the Pomo chief ended up with plates of beans and greens. Slocum wolfed his down, declaring it the best he had ever eaten. Li frowned, as if this praise was insincere, took their empty plates, and did not offer more.

"Who's behind it all in the camp?" Slocum asked aloud, more to himself than Daniel.

The skinny Indian perked up. "Who try destroying everything?" he asked. "I watch, I see, I—" Daniel clamped his mouth shut when the government agent came strutting into the tent. The short man sneered when he saw Daniel and Slocum. He stopped a few feet away.

"I need to know your authority for proclaiming yourself chief of the Pomo," Elliot said brusquely to Daniel. "Any treaty you sign will not be valid if you are not the duly elected representative of your tribe."

"What's the problem?" Slocum asked. "Is that other fellow giving you trouble again?"

"What other fellow?" asked Elliot, startled.

"Why, the warrior contesting Daniel's right to be chief."

"There's another one who says he is chief?" Elliot's voice was weak and surprise etched itself on his face.

"Daniel's the only elected chief. Ask any of the Pomo," Slocum said. He saw how the gaunt Indian appreciated this byplay.

"We cannot find them," Elliot said.

"Then which Pomo complained about the lumbering going on over their burial ground?" Slocum asked.

"That is a matter of record," Elliot said lamely. "Anyone can find out."

"Recorded down in Fort Bragg?" suggested Slocum.

"I—" Elliot sputtered. He swallowed, then said to Daniel, "I need written proof of your status as chief of your tribe."

"But the Pomo can't do that," Slocum said, beginning to enjoy the position Elliot found himself in.

"Why not?"

"That would steal away their souls. Every time a chief is selected, it is done by calling out the name of the man they want. Nothing's ever written down. You ought to know that."

"I must disallow your claim to be chief," Elliot said doggedly to Daniel, refusing to give up easily.

"Do it," Daniel said. "Do it and I declare war on all your people!"

"Don't meddle in tribal doings," Slocum suggested to Elliot, seeing that Daniel understood what was going on and was going along with the game.

"I will see what my, uh, superiors have to say about this."

"Keep peace with the Pomo. You know what that band of renegades is doing," Slocum said, a thought coming to him. "The chief's got his band of warriors out hunting for them."

"What?" Elliot seemed puzzled.

"The ones who shot up the train. Might even be the same bunch who ruined all our food in camp. Renegades. Chief Daniel's got his warriors out hunting them down. Soon as his men find them, he'll send you their scalps." Slocum saw Elliot turn white. The government man sputtered and left in a hurry.

"Why don't you see if you can't convince Li to fix you up with another plate of beans?" suggested Slocum. "I want to see where our government man runs to."

He waited a moment, then looked around the tent flap. Elliot hurried on his bandy legs across the camp, heading in the direction of the cabin used as an office. Slocum followed at a leisurely pace. There was no reason to intrude until he knew who all the players in this drama might be. He went to the rear of the cabin and pulled away some of the mud used to chink up the spaces between the fragrant redwood logs forming the wall. He pressed his face against the rough bark and peered into the dimly lit cabin.

Inside, Elliot paced nervously, wringing his hands and muttering to himself. Slocum felt rather than heard quick footsteps on the two steps leading into the cabin. He smiled when he saw Spence.

"What the hell's goin' on?" demanded the foreman.

"You tell me. I thought you said that Slocum was out of the way."

"He is. We saw to it. He was spyin' on us out in the forest and—"

"Like hell he's dead!" raged Elliot. "He's over in the mess tent with that damn fool Indian calling himself chief."

"I don't understand," Spence said. He perched on the corner of Gaynor's desk. "We got rid of Slocum, and Daniel's no chief. He can't prove it."

"As Slocum pointed out," Elliot said nastily, "we can't prove Daniel's *not* chief. And he's spun the yarn that the Indians doing all the dirty work are renegades, that Daniel's warriors are hunting them down to present us with their scalps!"

Spence said something Slocum didn't catch. He knew who was ultimately to blame for tying him to the log to die, but who had slugged him? Both of these owlhoots had been in the clearing. Until he found out, he didn't want to overplay his hand.

"What are we going to do? I want to get them out of here right now so we can start!" Elliot's voice almost broke with strain.

"We want the same thing, dammit," cursed Spence. "Don't go turnin' yellow on me. If we lose our nerve now, we lose everything we been workin' for."

"I know, I know. But what about Slocum?"

"I'll see to him personally," Spence said.

"He knows we're in this together. He watched us last night." Elliot sounded as if it were Spence's fault Slocum had trailed him to the clearing, but neither could know how little he had understood of their conversation.

"He's sticking around for a reason," Spence said. "And I think I know what it is." Spence turned grimmer still. He reached into a pocket and drew out a small Smith & Wesson. "No need to get fancy with him. I'll plug him in the back. Nobody'll be the wiser."

"You screw this up anymore and I—"

"You'll what?" Spence had turned downright nasty with his partner. Elliot backed down a mite when he saw the fury in the foreman's eyes. "You'll do as I say. We stick together, right? Right?"

"Yeah, sure," Elliot said with ill grace. "But you get rid of Slocum. Finish him off so he won't cause such a ruckus. I'll do what I can back in Fort Bragg to finish off the legal end of it."

"You do that," Spence said nastily. "You go on back so you don't have to get your hands dirty." The foreman watched Elliot leave. Slocum saw how Spence lifted the small hideout gun, pointed it at his partner's back, then lowered the pistol. Spence snorted in disgust and tucked the pistol away in a pocket before leaving the office.

Slocum walked around and saw Spence heading downhill toward where the logging crew worked on the next redwood giant. He wasn't sure what to do right now. If he turned his back on Spence, he was going to catch a bullet. On the other hand, he might be safest working with the crew. Whatever scheme Spence and Elliot had hatched, all the men couldn't be part of it.

But at least one was, he reminded himself. And that man had tied him to the redwood log to drown.

Slocum went to his tent and strapped on his gunbelt,

settling the weight of the Colt Navy on his left hip where it belonged. He had spent too long without his trusty six-shooter at his side. With Spence intending to back-shoot him at the first opportunity, Slocum wasn't going anywhere unarmed.

There only remained one question: What was he going to do now?

10

Slocum went a ways into the forest and settled down, watching the comings and goings from a secure spot high up in a scrub oak. Spence poked about, growling and grousing. The men pulled back from their foreman, obviously letting him vent his wrath—but not on them. Slocum knew the cause of the foreman's anger. He wanted to keep Spence off balance enough so the man made a mistake.

Slocum had questions to answer. Spence was part of it. So was Elliot. But what was their game? And who had slugged him when he eavesdropped on the pair? Slocum didn't much care if it had been his attacker or Spence and Elliot who had come up with the idea of tying him to the log and letting him drown. They were all equally guilty in his eyes. What he did not want to do was let any of the varmints get off scot-free.

He sat. He watched. He thought. But nothing came to him about why Elliot and Spence were in cahoots to drive the Fort Bragg Lumber Company out of business. If they worked for a competitor, what was the point? San Francisco needed all the lumber it could get and the builders there paid any amount for it. Squeezing the supply wasn't a likely reason. Did someone hate C. R. Johnson—or Ed Gaynor—enough to ruin the company? Slocum had the gut feeling Spence's motives had little to do with personal animosity.

Except toward him, and that was because of Faith looking kindly in his direction.

Thinking of the lovely redhead brought warm feelings to Slocum. If he helped her, he was also helping himself figure out who it was he had to get even with. He moved in the tree and repositioned himself to get a tad more comfortable. Slocum had no idea what he might see from his vantage point, but he wasn't seeing it. The men ate and turned in after cleaning and sharpening saws and tending other equipment for the next day's work. Spence vanished into his tent; Slocum reckoned the foreman was sleeping. Ed Gaynor was nowhere to be seen, but a light in the window of the cabin serving as office came on around dusk and did not waver.

He had seen no one go in or come out. That was the only thing out of the ordinary in the camp, so he went to investigate. Dropping to the ground, he winced as his entire body responded to the impact. Then the pain faded, and Slocum made his way across the camp to the cabin. Chancing a quick glance in the small window, he saw Faith bent over a book, working diligently entering numbers.

Slipping around to the front of the cabin, he went up the steps, lifted the latch, and entered quickly, closing the door behind him. No one had spotted him. So far. He turned to greet the woman, but Faith was so intent on her work she had not heard him enter. Watching her work was a simple pleasure, but one he appreciated. Short red hair swayed around her pale white oval face, framing her soft skin and lovely countenance perfectly.

"Good evening," Slocum said softly.

"Oh!" Faith jumped as if he had stuck her with a pin.

She dropped her pen and stared at him with wide blue eyes. She put one hand over her bosom and heaved a sigh of relief. "John, you scared the stuffing out of me!"

"I hope not," Slocum said, drifting closer. "From where I stand, it looks as if everything's still in all the right places." Delightfully so, in his opinion.

She smiled, and the light from her smile was greater than that cast by the kerosene lamp on the desk.

"I was working late, trying to get the books in order. Father has to go to the bankers. The company just isn't shipping enough timber to make expenses."

"Any idea why not?" Slocum asked, perching on the edge of the desk. From his vantage point he looked down on the pretty woman. He couldn't help noticing the upper buttons on her blouse had popped open, giving him a tantalizing view of the upper slopes of her creamy breasts. Faith was so wrapped up in her work she seemed oblivious of his lusting gaze.

"We don't have as many men working this month as we did last. That's part of it. And few of those who are working are very experienced." She heaved a sigh. The way her breasts rose and fell spurred a reaction in Slocum that he had to shift on the desk to hide from her. Faith was so intent, so focused.

"They're not working as fast," Slocum guessed.

"That's true. However, not every tree is the same. Some fall easily, others require far more work. So many factors come into play when it comes to output."

Slocum didn't answer. He stared at her now. Faith chewed at her lower lip, then locked eyes with him. She said nothing.

"You're about the prettiest woman I ever saw," Slocum said.

"And?" Faith said, a smile dancing on her lips.

"And I'd like to do something about the way I feel,

something that'll bring us both a peck of pleasure."

"Such as?" she said, leaning back in the chair and hiking her feet to the desktop. Slocum reached out and ran his fingers over her ankle, then worked higher, finding sleek, satiny white skin under the skirt. He moved closer, both hands stroking her thighs. Faith sighed again, this time with delight at what Slocum did for her.

"Oh!" She sat straighter when his fingers pushed aside her frilly undergarments and touched her nether lips. She gasped again when he thrust a finger into her moist wetness and began stroking in and out, slowly at first, and then faster when her inner lubricants slickened his finger.

"That's nice, John, but it's so . . . small. Have anything bigger to stuff into me?"

"What did you have in mind?" Slocum pulled his finger from her steamy core and moved still closer, dropping his gunbelt as he went. He needed to release his manhood from the cloth prison holding him in so painfully now. It took only a few seconds to pull open the buttoned fly and let out his meaty shaft.

"That's exactly what I had in mind," Faith said eagerly. She bent forward and put her mouth over him. The warmth and wetness of her sucking mouth was nothing compared to the way she used her agile tongue all over the purpled crown. He began burning as if a forest fire was raging within his loins. Reaching down, he tangled his fingers in her coppery hair and guided her head back and forth until he felt he couldn't stand it much longer.

Gently lifting, he moved her around so she sat on the desk, her legs spread and dangling down. Slocum moved into the vee as Faith pulled up her skirts and rolled them around her waist. She reached down and stroked along his shaft, moving from the base to the tip where her tongue had been so recently.

"Now, John, now," she said, gently drawing him forward. He moved and saw his length vanish into the crinkly, rust-colored furry triangle. For a moment, neither moved. Slocum relished the warmth and tightness all around him. When Faith leaned back on the desk, supporting herself on her elbows, this caused her female passage to collapse around him.

"So big," she cooed.

"So tight," he said. It felt as if she had lit the fuse that burned along his length to the powder keg buried in his balls. He bent forward, his mouth engaging hers. Then he started moving, slowly at first, twisting and turning and corkscrewing his way into her most intimate recesses.

The resolve to make this last quickly vanished. She was too much for him. Slocum began stroking faster, harder, deeper. The friction of his fleshy piston moving so erotically burned at his control. He kissed and licked at her throat and moved down lower, finding the tops of her breasts. Doing all he could to stimulate those fleshy melons only built both their passions to the breaking point.

"Oh, oh, ohhh!" Faith cried. She tensed as ecstasy seized her totally. She clamped down on his hidden shaft so hard Slocum thought she would crush him flat. He continued his in-and-out movement, speeding up now. Their groins met and ground together. Then he pulled out.

She began rising off the desk, giving as good as she got. Her legs lifted and she put her heels on the edge of the desk, giving her more leverage. Every time Slocum jammed forward, the sultry redhead rose from the desk and ground her hips in a big circle.

Slocum grunted and knew he could not go on much longer. He sped up, and Faith let out a new cry as her desires flooded forth. Then it was Slocum's turn to explode. After he geysered into her yearning cavity, he sank back into the chair and stared at the woman.

Her snowy cheeks were dotted with a hot red flush now. She sighed and opened her eyes.

"I could do that all night," she said.

"I wish I could," Slocum answered. She moved to the edge of the desk, her feet dropping to the cabin floor. Faith moved easily and straddled Slocum's waist, her privates pressing into his.

"You just might," Faith said, kissing him hard. She pulled back and grinned. "I can feel that you're going to try." Wiggling her hips back and forth, she settled down, letting him kiss and lick her breasts and lips and neck and ears.

Then it was time to start over again.

"When's your pa getting back?" Slocum asked. Faith murmured, still half asleep. They had not bothered leaving the cabin that served as an office for the lumber company. Her father had had a bedroll tossed into the corner to sleep on when he stayed in camp. It had suited them just fine, even if they had not gotten much sleep.

Faith stretched, her naked breasts flattening as her arms reached far above her head. She twisted like a contented cat, then snuggled closer to Slocum.

"He's due in on the morning train." This caused her to sit up suddenly. Dawn sunlight fell warmly through the easternmost window in the cabin. "Oh, no, he's due in any time now!" She pushed away the blankets and grabbed for her clothes. Slocum watched in appreciation as Faith dressed, smoothing out the wrinkles they had put in her skirt and blouse the night before.

He was slower to get his clothing on, but he spent a fair amount of time settling his six-shooter in its holster.

He had the feeling it would be folly to venture out into the camp without the Colt Navy swinging at his hip.

"Let's go meet him," Faith said. She saw how he hesitated. "What's wrong?"

"I don't think Spence'll cotton much to seeing us together." Slocum didn't bother telling her of Spence's promise to Elliot about shooting him in the back. Having the woman close by if the foreman opened up might prove too dangerous.

"Nonsense. He does not own me. No one does. I do what I want." She grinned impishly and added, "With whom I want!"

Faith opened the cabin door and hurried down the steps. Slocum followed, aware of dozens of eyes watching. The Chinese murmured among themselves, but the big response came from the direction of Spence's tent. The foreman was talking with Rufus and Lou. Spence pushed them aside and came storming over.

"You!" he bellowed, pointing his finger at Slocum. "Where the hell you been?"

"Around," Slocum said.

"You don't work, you don't get paid."

"So dock my pay," Slocum said. He saw Faith stop and come back, her long skirts swishing softly.

"I'll do more than that. You're fired, Slocum. Get the hell out of camp right now!" Spence was fit to be tied.

"Really," Faith said, miffed. "You can't go around doing things like that," she said. "My father will never approve. Mr. Slocum has been doing special tasks for him."

"And what kind of 'special tasks' has he been doin' for you?" Spence shot back.

"You are rude and crude, sir," Faith raged. "You will apologize immediately."

"Where'd you spend the night?" Spence demanded.

"Where'd *he* spend the night?" Spence read the answer on the woman's face. This only fed his anger. Slocum wasn't sure if it was because Spence considered Faith his exclusive territory, or because something more came into play. The foreman had tried to kill him, and might not wait until Slocum turned his back to try again. The bulge at Spence's right coat pocket showed where he had tucked in the small pistol.

The arrival of the train from Fort Bragg interrupted the argument. The engineer let out a long, loud screech on his whistle, and the grating of steel wheels spinning against tracks as the long train braked added to the cacophony.

"I'll see what Father has to say!" declared Faith, stamping her foot. She spun and stalked off. Slocum waited for Spence to go before trailing him. The foreman kept looking back over his shoulder as they climbed the hill to the ridge where the railroad tracks ran, as if he was worried Slocum might do to him what he had promised Elliot to do to Slocum.

The thought did cross Slocum's mind. A single round would end a great deal of the trouble in the Fort Bragg Lumber Company camp. But he held back. He knew it would only compound the woes raging all around and not give him the answer to questions he needed answered.

Who was the third man who had sent him down the river?

And what the hell was going on? Why were Spence and Elliot trying to drive the company out of business?

"Father!" cried Faith, rushing to throw her arms around his neck. Slocum saw what Faith did not. Ed Gaynor's drawn expression showed things were not going well. Whatever the result of his trip to San Francisco to ask the bankers for money, it wasn't all the man had hoped for.

"Dear, it's good to see you again," he said.

"Father, Spence wants to fire Mr. Slocum. Tell him he can't do it!"

"What?" Gaynor looked confused. "I don't know what you're going on about."

Faith unleashed a torrent of explanation, none of which made much sense to Slocum. Spence stood nearby, feet planted and his jaw clenched so tight his entire body quivered. Slocum watched him closely, in case he unleashed that anger and went for the pistol on his pocket.

"Hush, child," Gaynor said. "There's too much for me to take in all at once. I need to speak to you, find out what the books say. We need to have some serious discussions."

"This *is* serious, Father," the redhead insisted.

"No, no, I won't get involved," Gaynor said, holding up his hands and turning his head, as if to avoid seeing something unpleasant. "C. R. hired Spence to run the camp. He's an experienced logger and knows how to work a crew."

"But—"

"No buts. I'm sorry if Slocum and Spence didn't see eye to eye, but Spence's word is final."

"Get out, Slocum," the foreman said. "You heard Mr. Gaynor."

"Father!" Faith protested.

"It's all right, Miss Gaynor," Slocum said. "I never wanted to rile up folks."

"We'll talk about this, Father," the determined woman said.

"I'm sure we will. After I look at the financial information again." Gaynor glanced at Slocum, then hurried on his way without saying another word. Spence moved over and pushed out his chest, staring up at Slocum.

"You're going to be floating facedown in the river, Slocum. I guarantee it."

"You tried that once. What makes you think you'll do any better a second time?" Slocum asked. Spence reached for the pistol. If he had started to pull his hand out, Slocum would have cut him down then and there. And Spence realized it. The foreman glared, pushed Slocum out of his way, and stormed off, shouting at the lumberjacks to get to work.

Slocum let out a lungful of air he hadn't even known he was holding. Things had moved fast, and he wasn't sure what he ought to do now. But letting Spence, Elliot, and their unknown partner get away with trying to kill him wasn't going to happen.

"Slocum?"

He turned to see the train engineer standing behind him.

"You just got fired, right?" the man asked.

"Looks like it," Slocum allowed.

"What you planning on doing now?"

"A good question," Slocum said. "I wish I had a good answer. There must be a job over in Willits or back in Fort Bragg I can take." He didn't want to leave the area until he had settled accounts. Deep down, Slocum felt that when he got even with Spence and his cohorts, the Fort Bragg Lumber Company's problems would evaporate too.

"Might be I got an answer. Don't know how good it is." The engineer stared at the worn ebony handle of his Colt Navy. "I was driving the train when them Indians attacked the other day."

"Sorry about spooking you the way I did," Slocum said.

"Forget it. You're mighty good with that smoke wagon, aren't you?"

"Is the California Western Railroad looking for someone able to protect their rolling stock?" Slocum asked.

The engineer smiled and nodded. "Reckon I can give you a ride back to Fort Bragg so's you can talk with my boss. I told him about you, and he was impressed."

"But not so impressed he'd offer a reward," Slocum said.

"Mr. McGhee's a tight-fisted bastard," the engineer said cheerfully, "but he knows a good thing when he sees it. And I been bragging on you. The job of riding shotgun guard on my train's yours, if you want it."

Slocum did.

11

"Surely do feel better with you aboard, Slocum," the engineer said. He stuck his head out the side of the engine, yanked on the cord, and vented an ear-piercing shriek from the steam whistle. The train began moving sluggishly, then built power and made its way uphill and into the forested coast away from the town of Fort Bragg. Slocum had spent little enough time there. He had met with the superintendent of the California Western Railroad, who had taken the engineer's word about Slocum's abilities with a gun as gospel.

Slocum had found himself climbing back onto the train less than a half hour after being hired. Behind him in the wood tender lay two rifles, enough ammo to hold off an attack by every hostile Indian in Northern California, and two full bottles of rye whiskey.

"This standard issue?" Slocum asked, hefting one of the bottles of amber tarantula juice. He stared through it. At first he had thought it was clear. The sun revealed chunks of some foreign substance floating in it. Slocum didn't want to know.

"It's for me," the engineer said. "I get powerful thirsty runnin' into the woods. I get kinda shaky after Injun attacks too. I figger you're gonna run them red devils off a couple times, so that's celebratin' firewater too."

Slocum shook his head. The more he learned about the Indians in the area, the less he understood. Daniel was a Pomo, self-proclaimed. So were the five who had tried hunting him down. And so was the band hightailing it away from the coast, going inland to be away from all the furor kicked up by the railroad, the loggers, and the raiding Indians. Slocum hadn't gotten the feel that those Indians—Pomo?—who were heading for the Mt. Shasta area even knew the marauders.

What was gained by the occasional sniping at trains anyway? Slocum knew how valuable supplies were, but the Indians only slowed things down. What they stole was what they could carry off, hardly the act of organized resistance to the white man. More like bandits than Indians intent on ridding their land of unwanted tenants.

The government agent's claim that Pomo had approached him complaining that the lumbering was being done on burial grounds sounded farfetched too. Slocum wished Ed Gaynor had demanded to speak face-to-face with those wanting the Fort Bragg Lumber Company off the land rather than assuming Elliot knew what he was talking about.

If anything, most of the Indians were like Daniel—Chief Daniel—and hung around the camp scavenging what they could.

"Right purty country," the engineer said as they made their way across one bridge after another. "I could see putting a farm in here, if'n it weren't so hard clearing the land."

Everywhere Slocum looked, ten-and fifteen-foot-high stumps rose from monstrous sequoia already downed and taken into the Fort Bragg sawmills. It would take a trainload of dynamite to get rid of those burled stumps.

"Much blasting done on those stumps?" Slocum

asked, thinking how someone, probably Spence, had dynamited the redwood and brought it crashing down on his head.

"Not much. Some. The roadbed for the train is pretty easily cut, 'cept through some tunnels. We got a five-hundred-yard tunnel bein' blasted 'bout a quarter mile south of this line. When it's open we kin forget going over fifteen trestles. The wood from them alone'll pay for the tunnel."

"What do you mean?" Slocum kept a keen eye out for any sign of danger ahead. The day was peaceful and pleasant, the kind of day to while away sleeping in the sun.

"We don't leave them bridges up. We'll rip 'em out and sell the wood down in San Francisco. They're made from redwood, most of them. Good wood, tough, and smells agreeable too."

Slocum's mind drifted as the engineer rambled on. The work wasn't hard enough for the California Western to put on a fireman. The engineer handled both chores easily enough, even when the train headed uphill and along winding tracks plastered onto the side of steep canyon walls. At one point it was better than a hundred feet down to the meandering river. If the engine jumped the tracks there, it would be a watery death for everyone aboard, those that didn't die from the fall.

The engineer paid it no heed, and even sped up around some of the S turns, enjoying the day and the feeling of power driving such a powerful Baldwin engine gave him.

"What're we going back so fast for?" Slocum asked. "There's not a new log to ship down, is there?"

"We'd've taken it when we went back earlier," the engineer said. "Nope, we got some track work about three quarters the way to the logging camp. The crew needs ties. They was cut in Fort Bragg, and we're haulin' 'em back. Coals to Newcastle, that's the way it always seems."

"Easier to let the sawmill do the sawing," Slocum said, though he understood the man's point. Logs had to be moved from higher in the canyons to the coast, sawed, and then the ties shipped back. It seemed a fair amount of traveling for native wood to be returned to the forest where it once grew in such profusion.

"There's the crew," the engineer said. He let out a long, loud screech from the steam whistle, then began applying the brakes. The wheels dug into the steel rails and sent bright yellow and blue sparks flying in all directions. The heavy train slowed and came to a rest not fifty feet from the construction crew.

"Git them ties outta the freight car, Andy," the engineer called to the crew foreman. "If'n you need anything, lemme know and I'll fetch it on back next trip."

Slocum saw a half-dozen men sluggishly move toward the freight car, where the repair supplies had been stacked. He thought to help unload, but something warned him. It was an electric feel to the air, something like the way it feels before a spring thunderstorm out on the prairie. Not quite foreboding, but something powerful enough to make Slocum perk up and look around. He grabbed a rifle, clambered up the stacks of wood in the tender, and shielded his eyes, looking into the forest on either side of the tracks.

"You want a pull on this, Slocum?" called the engineer. He uncorked a bottle of whiskey and drained a couple fingers' worth.

"Stay in the cab," Slocum warned.

"What's wrong?"

"I don't know yet," Slocum admitted. He climbed to the rear of the tender, then jumped to the roof of the freight car fastened immediately behind. The passenger car had been left in the Fort Bragg rail yard to give the engine a better pull on the heavy freight car with its ties and spare rails.

Tugging his hat down low to shield his eyes, Slocum slowly turned, studying every shadow for movement. A light breeze whipped along the tracks, blowing the steam from the engine back in his direction. The hissing and creaking of the engine also masked any sounds he might otherwise have heard as an attack was suddenly launched.

Whoops and hollers of a half-dozen Indians caused Slocum to whirl about, bring up his rifle, and fire in one frantic move. His bullet went wide of the lead Indian, but that didn't matter. The Indian dug in his heels and came to a sudden halt, forcing two braves behind him either to dodge or plow into him.

This broke the back of the initial attack, giving Slocum time to lever in a new round. A second shot was better aimed and winged an Indian lifting a bow with a flaming arrow nocked. The Indian yelped as the hot lead burned a path across his chest, causing him to release the bowstring before he was ready. The flaming arrow arched high in the air, missing the side of the freight car. Slocum instinctively turned and watched as the arrow arched high over the train, then came plunging down on the other side of the freight car. The crew working to get ties from the car yelped in surprise and scattered.

The arrow had missed them by a country mile, but had accomplished its purpose nonetheless.

"From the north, Indians," shouted Slocum. "Maybe six of them. I wounded one." As he called out his warning, he fired with a deadly rhythm that drove the attackers back into the forest. When his Winchester's magazine came up empty, he jumped back to the tender and grabbed the other rifle. He pointed silently to the empty one, indicating the engineer should reload for him.

The man knocked back another inch of whiskey and then set to reloading, his fingers like giant clumsy sausages. Cartridges went all over the cab. Slocum was worried that a spark from the firebox might set off one. Then he was worried that he might not have enough firepower to drive off a concerted attack.

He was one man against at least a half dozen. If he had planned the assault, he would have split the force, half hitting the train from the north as a diversion for what the remainder did on the south side. Slocum swung from the cab and looked at the track crew. They had left the freight car and found refuge behind boulders and in gullies, waiting for the attack to be over.

They were easy targets. Or they ought to have been. Slocum saw no sign that the Indians were ready to launch an all-out attack from that direction. They weren't stupid; the instant Slocum started thinking they were he was a dead man. But why did they fight like this? It was almost as if they did not care if their assault worked.

"Time to take the fight to them," Slocum said, emptying his rifle into the woods to the north of the tracks. He tossed his empty rifle to the engineer, who had reloaded the first for him.

Slocum kept a sharp eye out for any sign of movement. Now and then a bush shook as if someone moved behind it. He fired into the undergrowth, not hitting anything.

"Here's the other rifle, Slocum." The engineer handed it to him, eyes wide and his face drawn.

"Take a sip or two of that rye for me," Slocum said, "but don't drink it all. I'll want some when I get back!"

With that he jumped from the cab, one rifle tucked under his left arm and the other ready to fire. Slocum plunged into the bushes and blundered about like a bull in a china shop. When he thought he'd made as much noise as he could, he dropped to his belly and waited, quiet as a mouse worried about a tomcat.

The combination of crashing and then silence had to draw the Indians like flies to shit. Slocum knew they could be patient. He was more patient. Long minutes passed. He saw slight movement ahead of him, but did not fire. He waited, hard as it was. More movement. Then two or three bushes shook as if wind brushed through the leaves. Finally, the top of a head poked up and down, prairie-dog style, intended to draw fire.

Slocum forced himself to relax.

The Indian showed himself and then stepped out into plain sight. Slocum drew a bead on him but held his fire. He was playing for bigger stakes. Two more Indians showed themselves. Another, and then the rest, all standing in a tight knot to discuss what was going on.

Slocum opened fire, levering in new rounds as fast as he could pull back on the trigger. The rifle barrel turned red-hot from the passage of so much lead so fast. He dropped the rifle, its melted barrel slightly askew now, and began firing the second as the Indians, no longer startled by the fusillade, took to their heels and ran like scalded dogs.

Hot lead followed them into the woods. Slocum doubted he had killed any of them, but not a one had escaped without a bloody groove cut by Slocum's bullets. More than one carried a slug in his chest or shoulder too. He knew that by the way they struggled to vanish into their woodland hideaway.

Slocum picked up the worthless rifle, hefted the still-good one, and pondered the wisdom of chasing them.

The Indians would leave a track any greenhorn could follow, but Slocum wasn't inclined to chase them down. He needed more equipment, in case they got smart and laid a trap or two for him along their trail.

He returned to the engine and climbed up.

"Ruined this one," Slocum said, tossing the rifle with the melted barrel into the wood tender. The engineer stared at him with eyes wider than saucers. "You got any of that rotgut left?"

The engineer silently thrust out a half bottle, as if Slocum was some kind of devil demanding his soul. Slocum drained a couple swallows, then wiped his lips.

"They skedaddled back into the woods. Decided not to hunt them down." Slocum took another sip of the whiskey. "You figure Mr. McGhee'll take the cost of another rifle out of my pay?"

The engineer froze for a moment, then laughed.

"Hell, Slocum, if he tries, *I'll* pay for a new gun for ya. The whole damned crew out there wettin' their pants'll buy you a goddamn *cannon* if you want!"

Slocum finished off the rest of the whiskey before the train returned to Fort Bragg.

"You deserve a bonus," McGhee said. "Don't have the money for it, so the best I can do is tell you to go relax and enjoy what pleasures you can find in Fort Bragg. I might say, there are a few delightful ones." McGhee gave Slocum a broad wink, then said in a loud whisper, "Try Miss Peggy o'er at the Sequoia House. She's 'bout the best there is in these parts."

"Thanks," Slocum said. He had nothing against Miss Peggy, but doubted she could hold a candle to Faith Gaynor when it came to amorous pursuits. But he could use the time in town before the railroad superintendent sent him out on another mission.

Stepping onto the main street, Slocum had to grab his Stetson to keep it from being blown off. The wind from the ocean proved brisk this afternoon. He walked down Main Street, looking for offices that had to be somewhere near. No boom town existed without at least a few rudimentary bureaucratic offices.

He smiled when he saw the land office behind the City Hill on Pine Street. This was exactly where he needed to do some browsing among the records.

The clerk behind the counter glanced up when Slocum walked in. The man had on a starched white shirt with forearms covered by thick black sleeve protectors to keep the ink from ruining his good clothing. A dozen ledgers lay around the man's desk as he transferred information from one book to the other and, from the stack of paper, to individual deeds.

"Help you, mister?" the clerk asked.

"Not sure," Slocum said. "Where are the county land deeds?"

"Those books yonder. Help yourself. If you need help, ask," he said insincerely, obviously hoping Slocum would vanish and let him return undisturbed to his paperwork.

Slocum began going through the plats, hunting for ownership of the land around the Fort Bragg Lumber Company's site. Bit by bit, he got closer, only to find the pages where the deed ought to have been recorded had been removed from the book. He rechecked the numbered pages. Three were cut out cleanly, as if a razor had been drawn down the inside to slice out the pages.

He doubted if the clerk knew anything about this. He closed the book and returned it to the sagging shelf along one wall.

"You need anything else?"

Slocum started to leave, then asked, "You know anything about the government agent? Elliot?"

"Old Jesse?" The clerk laughed. "He takes whatever job he can find, one right after the other."

"What was he before the government hired him?" Slocum asked.

"A half-dozen things. Most recently, he was an assistant over at the assay office."

"Do tell," Slocum said, leaving. He stepped into the bright afternoon sun glancing off the Pacific Ocean. The wind cut at his face, but he was feeling good. Some answers were beginning to suggest themselves to him.

12

Slocum stepped out into the cool, humid afternoon and decided it was time to get some grub. He and eating had been strangers since Spence had fired him. While Slocum did not miss Spence or the work required to fell a redwood, he did miss the regular food. Turning back toward the center of town to the south, Slocum went hunting for a cafe, but got sidetracked when he sighted the Bureau of Indian Affairs office on the far side of City Hall.

This might be where Elliot hung his hat, but something more drew Slocum. He smiled when he saw the small crowd circling Chief Daniel as the Indian climbed onto the stone steps and struck a pose like Abraham Lincoln speaking from the stump.

"My people will not be denied," he said, as if reading a rehearsed script. "The Pomo tribe has been held in captivity too long."

"Jist where are these Pomo?" asked someone in the crowd. Daniel withered the man with a cold look. The short Pomo drew himself up to his full five-foot height with a dignity that Slocum found compelling.

"There must be payment," he said.

Coming from inside the office, Elliot stood behind

Daniel for a moment, then said, "Uh, Chief, let's go in to my office and discuss this matter."

"No."

"No?" asked Elliot. "Why not? This is a bit public for what ought to be private negotiations."

"Why's that, Elliot?" called another heckler. "Ain't it our money you're dishin' out?"

"The U.S. government has not taken care of its children, the noble Pomo," Daniel said. Slocum found himself fascinated by the change in the Indian since being named chief. The one-time scavenger of garbage had found a spine. Slocum owed him his life, and now Slocum was willing to root for Daniel, as bogus as his claims were.

"We can arrange for food supplements," Elliot said hastily. "There can be—"

"We need more. My people starve in the midst of plenty."

"These things can't be done overnight," Elliot tried to explain. He got catcalls from the crowd. Daniel was being spurred on to make bigger demands of the government agent. Slocum found himself wondering at Elliot's game. Why deal at all with Chief Daniel? His bluff had been called when Ed Gaynor had randomly chosen Daniel and proclaimed him chief. Why didn't Elliot find some other way of getting whatever it was he wanted?

Or was playing along with Daniel getting Elliot his due?

"We are a proud and powerful people," Daniel said. "Do not think to rile us. You play with us, giving false promises. We will not permit it any longer."

"You're saying you'll go on the warpath?" Elliot's eyes widened in surprise. "We can deal, Chief Daniel. We can. You need supplies. I have some stored in a warehouse at the mouth of the Noyo River. We can get it upriver to your people."

"Money," hinted Daniel.

"Well, yes, uh, we can furnish a few dollars also. Just an initial payment from a larger amount due your tribe for the, uh, injustice your people have endured for so long."

"You givin' *him* money, Elliot?" asked one in the crowd. "Hell, I got Injun blood in my veins. Gimme some too!"

"Please. Chief Daniel is the representative of the Pomo Tribe."

"There's a dozen tribes out there callin' themselves Pomo," came the angry retort.

"In, please, Chief," Elliot said to Daniel. "We need to discuss this in private." Elliot glanced at the crowd, now growing angry. They saw money being handed out and wanted some of it, for whatever reason they could think up.

"You get some firewater too, Danny boy!" shouted a man at the rear of the crowd. "I'll be glad to help you drink it!" This produced a round of laughter that broke the tension. Some began drifting away, taking the wind out of the sails of those remaining. Grumbling, they left.

Elliot heaved a sigh, took Daniel by the elbow, and steered the man into his office. Slocum wished he could overhear what Elliot promised Chief Daniel for his tribe. It probably amounted to a small fortune, certainly more than Daniel had seen in his short lifetime.

The government agent's willingness to appease Daniel while other bands of Pomo still raided puzzled Slocum. Did Elliot want to keep down the level of violence at any cost? Shaking his head, Slocum went to find a cafe to appease his hunger. In two hours, he was back in the cab of a California Western Railroad engine heading up into the redwood forest again.

"Surely is dark out here, ain't it?" asked the engineer. The man pushed back his striped cap and wiped sweat from his forehead. He had been feeding the firebox and trying to drive the train on an uphill grade. The two jobs almost proved more than he could handle, but Slocum wasn't going to help out. Not only did he not want to break his back shoveling the wood into the boiler, but he wanted to keep a sharp eye out along the tracks.

McGhee had been worried about all Chief Daniel had said in public, and even more about what Elliot might give him—or not give him. The railroad superintendent felt this might cause more friction between the Indians and the loggers, not to mention the crews working on the California Western Railroad leading to the lumber camp. Slocum tried to point out the raids had begun long before Daniel had been promoted to chief, but stopped short of telling McGhee about the con being worked by Ed Gaynor on the government agent.

McGhee had been positive some devilment would occur on the next run, and had assigned Slocum to act as shotgun guard.

In the cab, Slocum felt as safe as could be. He had the remaining Winchester, ammo for it, and a long-barreled shotgun that ought to be good for bringing down Canadian geese—all the way north in Canada. With the scattergun in hand, he felt he could take out a small army, should one appear.

"Good place for an ambush," Slocum allowed. Try as he might, he saw nothing out of the ordinary. The game in the forest had long since gotten used to the hissing and puffing of the steam engine as it passed through their domain. The birds didn't stop chirping in the day, and the nocturnal animals hardly growled at the iron horse interrupting their hunt.

Slocum reacted instinctively, the long shotgun barrel coming up smoothly. He hesitated pulling on the double triggers when he saw an owl outlined against the brightly starred night sky. He relaxed. McGhee had put him on edge for no good reason. The Indians doing all the raiding, and Slocum decided he might as well call them Pomo, never had their hearts in the fight. Their planning was always poor, and they turned tail and ran at the first sign of opposition.

As far as he could tell, the Pomo had never really stolen much from the California Western. Chief Daniel had probably begged more off the Fort Bragg Lumber Company than any of the marauders had swiped as a result of their raiding.

He idly wondered if Daniel knew the warriors raising the ruckus and if he would try to stop them now that he was "chief." Slocum doubted it. Daniel might not be able to find the raiders, much less exert any control over them. Slocum smiled wryly, remembering how the five had chased Daniel and how terrified he had been of them.

Their number had been reduced a little, but Slocum wondered how they recruited. From the scattered bands of Pomo all around the area? Or did the new recruits simply show up, like iron filings to a magnet?

"Need to find the magnet," he murmured.

"How's that, Slocum?" called the engineer. He wiped away more sweat and sat on the drop seat on the right side of the cab. He peered out, trying to make out the tracks ahead illuminated by the powerful lamp. Mostly, the California Western did not run at night, but supplies were desperately needed at a trestle repair job. If the bridge collapsed, the town of Willits and the Fort Bragg

Lumber site would be cut off until it was rebuilt. Maintaining it would be far easier than rebuilding.

"Nothing," Slocum said. "What's the matter with this bridge?"

"The one we're dropping supplies off for?" The engineer scratched himself through his bib overalls. "Crew didn't blast right for the foundation. Put one of them danged footings on soft dirt, so's the entire structure is 'bout ready to collapse."

"Intentionally?"

The engineer snorted in contempt. "Them fellas buildin' the bridge are too stupid to do somethin' like that intentional. They jist took the easy way out and never asked, that's all."

Slocum had seen that happen too many times. If the foreman turned his back for an instant, mistakes were made. And if the foreman wasn't too bright, he supervised the blunders. Whatever had happened to this particular bridge sounded like stupidity rather than purposeful destruction.

"How much farther?" asked Slocum.

"Hold yer horses, Slocum," the engineer said. "We got three more bridges and a couple S turns to get through." Finally, the train slowed as the engineer carefully negotiated the last few hundred yards, stopping just short of the bridge.

"Hate like hell, but I'll have to back down the mountain till I get to the turnaround at Northspur. Danged fools," the engineer grumbled.

Slocum carried the shotgun in the crook of his left arm as he dropped to the ground and walked forward. The track was in good condition. For all he could see in the dark, the bridge seemed sturdy enough, but he wasn't going to ask the engineer to test it out. He trusted the man's skill and experience in such matters.

"Hello!" Slocum called. "Where are you hiding?"

The engineer came out and stood beside him. "Now that's peculiar. Them fellas is supposed to be here waitin' fer us."

Slocum poked around, hunting for the repair crew. He found a camp with a cooking fire dead for better than a few hours. The few charred logs in the fire pit were cold. Some of the crew's equipment lay scattered around. He couldn't tell if their packs had been searched or if they were just messy.

"It's like they jist upped and left," the engineer said.

"Might be they're working on the bridge," Slocum said.

"Danged dangerous if that's so. Cain't see a thing." The engineer returned to the tracks and walked out a few yards, peering over the verge at the fifty-foot supports holding bridge and track.

"See anyone?"

"No light. They weren't good enough to build it right in the daylight. Cain't imagine them doin' it right in the dark." The engineer took off his striped cap and scratched his head, then went to the edge and took a leak over the side.

"If they're below, that'll get their attention," Slocum said wryly.

"Nobody home. Danged strange." The engineer seemed tossed on the horns of a dilemma. Slocum solved the problem for him.

"If you don't mind some more work, let's unload the steel work and the tools."

"Cain't leave valuable equipment untended," the engineer said. "Mr. McGhee'd have my head for it."

"We unload and I stay to guard it until the crew shows up. You go on back, ask McGhee what he wants to do. If he sends out a new crew at first light, and the other folks have shown up, they get the work done twice as fast. And if they haven't put in an appearance, the new crew gets the pleasure of finishing the chore."

"That's fine by me," the engineer said, obviously ill at ease. He looked into the dark woods on either side of the track, as if expecting grizzly bears to attack.

It took Slocum and the engineer almost two hours to get the heavy steel supports and the other equipment off the freight car and dropped near the tracks.

"You be all right, Slocum?"

"Leave me one of your bottles, and I'll be fine," Slocum said. The engineer tossed down a half-full bottle of rye, which Slocum caught easily. He put it beside the Winchester and the mound of ammo from the train. Waving with the shotgun, he bid the engineer a good trip back down to the coast.

The long white streamers of steam from the stack vanished around a lower S curve, and finally even the distant rumble of steel on rail faded into the night. Slocum was alone. Very alone.

He made a circuit of the camp, trying to find where the repair crew had gone off to. The soft ground was chopped up by a lot of boots and maybe a moccasin print or two, but Slocum could not be certain. Which direction the men had taken remained a mystery to him as he circled the camp twice more. They might as well have been sucked up to the moon for all he could tell.

Slocum settled down at the edge of the camp, not bothering to build a new fire. He preferred to listen to the forest sounds around him, to the river murmuring fifty feet below, to the clues that would alert him if anyone tried sneaking up.

A quick sip now and then from the engineer's bottle kept Slocum awake and warm and alert enough so he noticed a sudden diminishing of night sounds from back

down the tracks. He hefted the shotgun, stuffed a handful of shells into his coat pocket, and moved to get a
better view of the equipment piled by the tracks.

He crouched in shadows, waiting for something to
happen. A half-moon had risen, casting pale silver light
onto the tracks. At first, Slocum thought he was imag-
ining things. Then he saw an Indian decked out in war
paint moving slowly along the tracks. A second warrior
followed, and then two more came.

"Four?" he wondered. If he fired both barrels of the
shotgun, he could take them all out. That wasn't what
Slocum wanted, even if it did successfully defend the
California Western property.

He wanted answers, not dead bodies.

The four warriors came on more boldly and stood by
the equipment, easy targets. Either they had dispatched
the repair crew already or knew the camp was deserted.
Slocum wanted to find out which it was. He started moving, stumbling a little in the dark. The small noises he
made did not attract the warriors' attention. They were
too intent on digging through the mound of equipment
hunting for something worth stealing.

Slocum raised his shotgun and came up on the Indians
from behind. They were silhouetted plainly in the bright
moonlight. The sound of the double hammers cocking
brought the four men around, hands grabbing for knives
and pistols jammed into their waistbands.

"Move and I'll cut you all in half," Slocum said
loudly.

He cursed when they split into two groups, one running into the forest and the other sprinting for the bridge.
Firing one barrel to keep the ones heading for the forest
running, he spun, lowered his aim, and fired at the second pair. One yelped and crashed to the ground, heavy
buckshot pellets in his legs. The other put his head down

and ran faster, crossing the bridge and vanishing on the far side before Slocum reached the wounded Indian.

"Don't move," Slocum ordered. He had his Colt Navy out, cocked and aimed at the man's face. The Pomo subsided, his expression a combination of fear and contempt.

Slocum rolled the man onto his belly and examined his legs. They were a bloody mess, but no real harm had been done. Only three pellets had hit him, one in the right calf and the other two in his left buttock. He might not sit for a spell, but otherwise he wasn't badly hurt.

"You and I are going to have a little talk," Slocum said, sinking cross-legged to the ground by the Indian. The Pomo pretended not to understand, but Slocum saw that he did. He certainly understood when Slocum leveled his six-shooter and pulled the trigger. The Indian screeched in fright as the .36-caliber slug tore off the top of his left ear.

"Missed, but not by much. Think I can shoot off your other ear?" Slocum cocked the pistol again and slowly swung it to the other side of the man's head, making sure he lingered when the barrel was pointed directly between his eyes.

"Don't," the Pomo said, his voice edged with fear.

"Why not? You tried to rob the railroad of its equipment. For all I know, you killed the repair crew already."

"They ran off. We no kill. They run!"

"Like your friends?" Slocum asked, emphasizing how alone the brave was. "Why not tell me what you were doing here?"

"Steal," the Pomo said. "We were told to steal. To shoot and take what we wanted."

"You were being paid to steal from the California Western Railroad?"

The sullen expression on the Indian's face gave Slocum the answer to his question more eloquently than words could.

"Who's paying you to make life hell for the railroad?"

The Indian said nothing. Slocum fired again, taking off a bit of hair from the right side of the Indian's head but missing his ear.

"Damn, missed," Slocum said, cocking his six-gun again.

"He pay us good."

"Who's he?"

"Dunno name. Big fella in town. Proper *tyee*."

Slocum knew that meant something equivalent to chief. What he did not know was who the Indian meant.

"Describe him."

By the time the Pomo had finished, Slocum was sure the government agent was responsible. It didn't surprise him unduly, but what did Elliot—and Spence—hope to gain from bedeviling the railroad?

That was something he couldn't find out from the Pomo.

"You don't know where the repair crew is? You didn't do anything to them?"

The Indian shook his head in vigorous denial. Slocum let down the hammer on his Colt and motioned for the Pomo to take off. He had learned all he was likely to from the man.

For a moment, the Indian hesitated, expecting Slocum to shoot him in the back. Then he hobbled faster and dived into the woods, vanishing without a trace. The Indian might be gone, but what remained were some knotty questions Slocum was still hard-pressed to answer.

But answer them he would.

13

Slocum dozed the rest of the night, the shotgun at his elbow. More than once a lovelorn wolf howled and brought him up, hand reaching for the gun. Then he slipped back to a troubled sleep, dreaming of Chief Daniel and Elliot and Spence and Faith Gaynor and trying to make some sense out of the stew pot of puzzle pieces. The only thing he got from the light sleep was a kink in his neck.

Somewhere around nine a.m. the tracks began vibrating. Ten minutes later he saw the long white plume of steam rising from the locomotive's smokestack. Then he was waving to the engineer, who expertly brought the train to a halt not ten feet from the bridge.

"You see any of them varmints, Slocum?" the engineer called.

"The other crew?" Slocum shook his head. He had no idea what had become of them. The attacking Pomo might have run them off. They might have taken it into their heads that getting drunk was a better way to live than freezing to death in the coastal mountains of California and working on a piddling little bridge. Or Elliot might have bought them off, the way he was trying to do with Chief Daniel.

"Damnation, that's what I feared," the engineer said. "I got three men off another crew. That's not enough to reinforce the damn bridge."

"Let 'em try," Slocum suggested. He had worked as a carpenter and could help, if someone knew enough to tell him where to fix beams and put in other supports. But he wasn't going to join the work crew unless he had to. The injuries he had accumulated were healing, but he still had a twinge now and again in his leg. The cuts on his back were mostly healed, but the skin itched and gave him the golly-wobbles if he reached too high above his head.

"Not much else we kin do," the engineer said. "Git on in. We're headin' back to Fort Bragg. No reason to sit here burnin' wood all the livelong day."

Slocum swung up and deposited his arsenal behind in the wood tender. The engineer sniffed the cordite.

"Had a couple visitors last night," Slocum said.

"Two- or four-legged?"

"What's the difference?" Slocum asked, sitting on a small drop seat. The engineer unloaded the half crew, got his engine reversed, and started back down the tracks until he reached the Northspur turnaround. It took the better part of an hour for the engineer to accomplish the turn, taking a fair amount of time to talk to the man at the small station and a woman Slocum figured was the stationmaster's daughter. Slocum joshed the engineer all the way back to Fort Bragg about being sweet on the woman.

"Aw, go on. I was jist bein' polite," the engineer said. But the broad smile told Slocum there was more to it than simple civility. Slocum's mind drifted as they rushed back to Fort Bragg, passing through redwoods and spruce and a dozen other kinds of trees Slocum could not identify. Mostly, he thought of Faith and the trouble at the lumbering camp. He hoped she was all right. It looked more and more as if Elliot and Spence would turn violent if they didn't get what they wanted, their ire turning against Ed Gaynor and maybe even his daughter.

Slocum waved to the engineer as he dropped off the locomotive where the railroad tracks crossed Main Street at Pine. It was getting to be a routine with him. Every time he had a few minutes off, he sought food. But this time, it being past noon, he decided a cold beer might go good with food. Hunting, he finally found a saloon serving a decent lunch of beef sandwiches along with the nickel beer. He had settled in the corner of the room, munching happily, when he heard voices he recognized.

Glancing over his shoulder, Slocum saw Elliot guiding Chief Daniel to a small private room at the rear of the saloon. The government agent whispered urgently to the Pomo chief, going on and on about something Daniel obviously did not want to hear.

"No," Daniel said. "This is not right. My tribe should benefit, not just me."

This surprised Slocum, unless Daniel was running some kind of confidence game on Elliot. Daniel had been little more than a scavenger when Ed Gaynor tapped him to be chief. Now Daniel sounded like a real chief with the concerns of his tribe placed ahead of his own personal needs.

Slocum picked up his beer and half-eaten roast beef sandwich and made his way to a table near the doorway to the back room, which turned out not to be as private as Elliot surely hoped. Leaning back, Slocum put his ear only a few inches from the door and a few feet from the government agent.

"How can you help your people if you are personally suffering?" asked Elliot, apparently angling for a way to convince Daniel he ought to take what was probably a sizable bribe. "Here, have a drink."

"I cannot afford whiskey," Daniel said.

"Don't worry about it. We're friends and friends do for one another. I'll buy today. Barkeep!" he called outside. "Bring us a bottle of your special stock!"

The barkeep reached under the bar, pulled out an amber-filled bottle that might actually have been bourbon, and headed for the room. As the bartender came back out, Slocum grabbed his arm.

"That stuff any good? What you gave them?" Slocum jerked his thumb in the direction of Elliot and Daniel.

"Best we got. You want a shot? Fifty cents."

"Whew, powerful expensive," Slocum said.

"Powerful whiskey," the barkeep replied.

"Give me a shot," Slocum decided. He watched the barkeep pour a shot out of a bottle filled with similar liquor. Slocum knocked back the shot and whistled. "You weren't kidding about it being powerful stuff. That's got the kick of an angry mule."

He knew Daniel wasn't going to drink more than two or three shots without getting roaring drunk—which had to be what Elliot intended.

Slocum got more interested in what the government agent wanted from the Pomo chief.

"Yes, Chief Daniel," Elliot went on in a soothing voice, "you got responsibility to more than yourself now, and I'm glad to see you are addressing the problems of your people. Drink up."

Slocum heard Daniel gulp as he swallowed another couple ounces of the potent liquor.

"I like this," the Indian said, his voice husky from the effects of the whiskey on his throat.

"Good, good. Have some more. Now," Elliot said, his voice lowering so Slocum could hardly hear, "consider my proposal. It'll mean fifty whole dollars for you."

"What 'bout my tribe?" Daniel asked, his words fuzzy around the edges from the firewater. "Need t-to th-think of th-them."

"This *is* for your tribe, Chief," Elliot said, his voice increasingly cajoling. "All you need do is file the charges against Ed Gaynor. You don't owe him anything."

"He make me chief," Daniel said, but Elliot wasn't listening. He was too intent on his own agenda.

"Gaynor's a fraud. He's logging on the burial grounds for your people. Can the Pomo permit this indignity to continue? No!"

"No?"

"No," Elliot said forcefully. "You're a chief. You have to stand up to the white man. Let me file the protest with the U.S. Government for you. We'll have the lumbering stopped within a week and have them out of your woods, the land belonging rightfully to the Pomo Indians, by this time next month."

"Why sh-should I do that?" asked Daniel.

"Fifty dollars is yours," Elliot said, a serpent in the Pomo chief's Garden of Eden. "And your tribe gets the white man away from your sacred land."

"Don't b-bury our dead," Daniel protested. "Burn on pyre, spread ashes in r-river."

"But this land is where you find the wood for those pyres, right?"

"Yes."

"That's it!" cried Elliot. "They're taking sacred wood and not paying you. They should be kicked off the land right away. Here, Chief Daniel, have another drink. We can sign the papers in a while back in my office."

Slocum had heard enough. Daniel was drunker than a lord and hardly knew where he was, much less what scheme Elliot was prodding him into. Slocum stopped at the bar and motioned the barkeep over.

"Does Elliot come in here often with his Indian clients?"

The barkeep shook his head. "Never seen him with an Injun before, here or anywhere. We don't like them in here and don't serve 'em," the barkeep said. Slocum knew he meant the Indians. "That's why I put Elliot in the back room." The barkeep reached under his stained apron and pulled out a thick wad of greenbacks. He grinned, then stuffed it back into his pocket.

Slocum realized anything could be bought with enough money. The only question he had now was why Elliot wanted the land where the Fort Bragg Lumber Company worked cutting down the trees.

"Don't blame you, Slocum," the engineer said, slowing for a bend in the track. "The way you left the logging camp, there's no reason for you to poke your nose back. You might get it chopped off."

The bridge had been repaired, the line between Fort Bragg and Willits open again and, as far as Slocum could tell, safe. The freight the California Western now hauled up from the coast consisted mostly of two steam donkeys for dragging big trees up the side of the mountain. That told Slocum that Spence had already cut the sequoias down lower, near Pudding Creek, and now had to worry the newly felled trees up to the railroad for shipment to the sawmills.

"Pick me up on the way back," Slocum said, jumping from the train before it gained speed again. He hit the ground hard, ran a few steps, then slowed. He waved to the engineer, then headed into the forest before someone spotted him.

Slocum hiked for twenty minutes before he heard the

loud shouts, the curses, and the rhythmic sawing sounds of a logging crew working on a giant redwood. He veered away from them and headed for camp. If he wanted answers, the best time to get them was when Spence and the others were gone. In a way, Slocum hoped he caught sight of the lovely red-haired Faith again. But he had to satisfy his own curiosity—and get some revenge on the men who had tried to kill him.

The camp was like a calm ocean surface. Slocum knew that just beneath the serene top boiled furious activity. The Chinese worked at laundry, chopping wood, and cooking chores. Indians moved through the camp like copper-skinned ghosts, poking here and there and being chased off by Li when they got too close to the cook tent. Once Slocum saw Faith with her father in the cabin they used as an office.

Ed Gaynor had aged a dozen years. He appeared gaunt and his hands shook just a mite when he took a sheaf of papers Faith handed him. Slocum didn't get a good look at her before she and her father closed the door behind them. From the set of her shoulders and the way she walked, he thought a powerful load was being heaped on her too.

Drifting like a puff of smoke, Slocum made his way through the camp, unseen by anyone, even the scavenging Indians. At Spence's tent, he ducked inside and pulled the flap down to give himself a tad more privacy as he rummaged through the foreman's belongings. Not sure what he sought, Slocum set to the task of searching everything.

Hidden under the man's bedroll stretched out on the cot, a scrap of paper caught Slocum's attention. He held up the paper and tried to make out the words. The printing was too faded, but the weaving lines appeared to be a topographical map. Turning it over and over, Slocum tried to align it with some feature of the canyon where the logging went on even as he poked around in Spence's gear. The best he could figure, the line down the center portion of the map was the creek that ran down to the coast. In a couple of places, Spence had drawn in an X, then done a poor job of erasing it, leaving behind inky smears.

"What the hell!"

Slocum dropped the paper and spun to face the foreman. Spence's surprise kept him from reacting as fast as Slocum. With a punch designed to fell one of the big redwoods, Slocum reared back and unloaded a blow that sent Spence staggering.

Rather than stay and fight, Slocum lit out, stepping over the fallen foreman and darting for the thickest part of the forest.

"Hey, thief, stop 'im," gasped Spence. "Stole from me. Thief!"

The denunciation rang in Slocum's ears as he dodged, then hit a game trail, and ran as hard as he could. Less than a hundred yards down the narrow dirt path, he jumped, caught an overhanging limb, and pulled himself up. Making like a squirrel, he jumped from one low limb to another until he reached a stand of pines, with high limbs and sticky trunks.

Slocum dropped back to the ground, hunting for hard sections of dried earth or rocks to jump onto. He did everything he could to avoid leaving a trail Spence could follow. Then, when he was sure he had totally hidden his trail, Slocum doubled back to be certain.

He sucked in his breath when he saw his aerial acrobatics had not thrown Spence off his trail at all. What had slowed the foreman, now brandishing a rifle, was the man's careful stepping from rock to rock. Slocum hunkered down and waited to see if Spence persisted or went back to camp in defeat. What he did startled Slocum again.

The foreman ran his fingers up and down the rifle stock, but neither went back nor advanced. He paced around the spot where he had lost the spoor, as if he was waiting for something.

Slocum considered moving on. He had a good idea where the Xs on the map might be. He could explore them firsthand while Spence wasted time dithering in the forest, but something held him to the spot. Spence's behavior struck him as odd, and he wanted to find out what was going on.

"Aieee!"

The war whoop came from behind him. Slocum reacted instinctively, bending forward and corkscrewing to the side. A heavy body crashed into him, and he felt strong hands groping to circle his neck in a death-grip. Twisting around hard, Slocum threw off the Pomo warrior trying to strangle him. The Indian landed hard on the ground, the air knocked out of his lungs. Slocum wasted no time falling down, driving his knee into the man's chest.

The Indian passed out from the shock. But the damage had been done. Spence had been alerted. Worse, Slocum saw three other Pomo warriors coming at him through the gathering dusk.

"There he is!" shouted Spence. "Get him. Take the son of a bitch's scalp!"

Slocum snatched the knife from the fallen brave's belt and threw it at an attacking Indian. The deadly knife missed its target in the center of the Pomo's chest, but did cut his right arm, producing a squall of pain that diverted the others for a brief instant.

Not looking back, Slocum ran deeper into the woods. He had come hunting for some reason why Spence and

Elliot wanted this land. Maybe there was a burial ground around somewhere, one he had never seen a trace of. But he did have solid proof that Spence was in cahoots with the Indians causing all the trouble along the California Western Railroad line. Gaynor might not do anything about his foreman, but McGhee wasn't likely to ignore someone destroying his rolling stock and burning his bridges.

"There he goes," Spence shouted. "After him. Ten dollars to the one of you that kills him!"

The words gave Slocum a beacon in the night to use for his own benefit. He cut to his right, then right again, doubling back toward Spence. Cut off the head and the body dies, his old sniper training reminded him. If Spence was taken out of the fight, the Pomo would give up and go away.

"Where he go?" demanded one Indian. "I do not smell him!" The man sniffed the air like a hound dog hunting a coon. Slocum hoped the salve Li had given him for his leg had long since given up its distinctive odor.

He froze for a moment, letting the Indian walk past him, missing him by yards. Then Slocum advanced again, heading for Spence. The foreman stood nervously fingering his rifle trigger, twitching from one side to another at the slightest sound in the forest.

Three Indians were seeking Slocum. One lay unconscious where he had failed in his attack. Slocum counted them as all out of the fray. Only Spence remained. Slocum advanced a few more feet, then sank down to be certain of his prey.

"I hear him!" shouted Spence. "He's back here, you fools!"

Slocum wasn't sure if this was a ploy to smoke him out or if Spence really had heard him. Slocum gauged distances, got his feet under him, then dived forward.

He staggered a few paces, then leveled out and tackled the foreman, bringing him down hard.

As he knocked Spence to the ground, the man's rifle discharged. The explosion echoed through the still forest and drew back the three Indians.

Slocum cocked his fist back and let it fly. He caught Spence on the side of the head, knocking him out, but the sounds of the three returning Indians convinced him to hightail it.

Dashing into the woods, Slocum used every bit of frontier lore he had ever learned to conceal his trail. And it was needed. The three Indians after him were good trackers—and determined to kill him for the reward Spence had offered.

14

After twenty minutes of dodging the Indians, Slocum was worried that he might have indeed found the burial ground everyone was so intent on finding. Unfortunately for him, it would be wherever the Indians caught up with him. Every trick he had learned from Cheyenne and Apache, from Sioux and Navajo, had failed him as he dodged through the sequoia forest. The Indians knew the woods too well for him to throw them off his trail easily. He needed a diversion to put some distance between them and him. Most of all, he needed time to catch his breath and try to figure out the best way of getting the hell out of there.

"He's over here," called Spence's harsh, grating voice. "I can hear him suckin' wind!"

Slocum held his breath, waiting for his pursuers to burst into the clearing in front of him and point rifle and bow and arrow at him. But Spence led them astray. Slocum let out his pent-up breath slowly, his grateful lungs relaxing from the strain.

He had a few minutes while the foreman led the Indians on a wild-goose chase. He doubted he had more time than that. The Indians were the ones attacking the train. Of that he was sure, but now they were fiercer and more determined. He had run them off with a few well-placed shots before. Slocum had the feeling now that he would have to put them into their graves before they stopped coming after him.

And maybe not even then. He wondered if there really was a Happy Hunting Ground—and if the Indians would continue to hunt him down for all eternity.

"You go first," Slocum vowed. "I'll be along later. Much later." Grimly setting out, he made his way downhill, that being the only direction he could go with any assurance of finding his way back later. He had lost track of where the railroad ran through the woods, and needed to get his bearings from the rapidly flowing creek before hitching a ride back into Fort Bragg.

He had not thought much of the tiny coastal town before. Now it seemed like paradise to him.

Slocum took long, carefully placed steps, walking over bushes and trying to plant his boots where the imprint in the soil would be hidden by branches and vines. Sometimes he succeeded. Other times he failed. But always he made his way lower on the mountain, homing in on the soothing rush of water in Pudding Creek.

As he went, he studied the ground carefully for any sign of a burial ground. Slocum doubted he could find it by accident, and there had not been any gossip about one in the logging camp. Men like the loggers would dig up every grave, hunting for trinkets and souvenirs. If they found a broken knife or an arrow buried alongside the body, there would be boasting and bragging about the biggest Indian massacre in the history of the West. Slocum had heard nothing like that passing among the loggers. Moreover, any silver trinkets or beadwork would have been proudly displayed as trophies showing the bearer's fighting prowess.

The lumberjacks had done nothing of the sort while

sitting around their campfire, and Slocum had to believe they had not blundered across an Indian cemetery during their work.

He reached the bottom of the hill and stood a dozen feet from the rushing creek. The sound of the running water covered any small noise he might make as he plowed his way up the bank, his feet sucking in the mud, but it also covered any noise his trackers might make. Slocum got jumpier by the minute, looking back over his shoulder far too often for comfort.

"Relax," he told himself as he dropped into the shelter of a burned stump and wiggled back, the lightning-charred wood protecting him on three sides. Looking up, he saw tall trees masking the rising three-quarter moon. And in front of him ran the creek. He was blind in several directions, but also safe enough for the moment to rest and get his thoughts in order.

Finding the ceremonial ground was not likely to happen by accident. Slocum pictured the map Spence had hidden in his gear, wondering if that might be an attempt to mark off where the burial ground was. He shook his head, remembering what Daniel and others had said.

Like the Klamath, the Modoc, and other Northern California Indian tribes, the tribes that made up the Pomo did not bury their dead. He was hunting for a phantasm. So why was Elliot so intent on having Chief Daniel say the Pomo resented having Gaynor and his crew logging over a nonexistent burial ground?

The answer had to lie under one of the Xs on Spence's map. Slocum wished he had brought it with him, but in the scuffle getting out of the foreman's tent he had dropped the scrap of paper. All he had to go on was his memory.

Slocum dozed, coming awake now and then when he heard something unusual out in the forest. More often than not, he spotted deer coming to the water to drink. Once he heard a grizzly roaring in the distance. He hoped it had found itself a good meal in three Indians and a logging foreman.

Slocum checked his watch after another short snooze and saw it was almost two in the morning. The moon had slipped behind heavy clouds. Along with the thick canopy granted by the towering sequoias, it was darker than inside a cougar's belly. Slocum slid from his protective stump and stretched. He needed more of Li's wonderful unguent for his leg, but otherwise, he felt as if he could whip his weight in wildcats.

Making his way along the bank, being sure he walked on rock or where the rushing water would erase his tracks, he went downstream until he came to a flat area where the loggers had brought dozens of their biggest trees. Smaller trunks lay on the soft ground and had been used as rollers to slide the redwoods into the water.

Slocum went cold inside remembering that he had been tied to one of those trees and then sent on his way downriver to Fort Bragg. Someone would pay. Spence and Elliot and someone else.

He canted his head to one side and listened for any sound that might betray Spence or the Indians. Hearing nothing, Slocum made his way up the hill, found a trail cut by the lumberjacks, and soon entered the sleeping camp. A smile came to his lips when he heard the noise echoing out of the men's tents.

They sawed wood all day—and all night too. Their raucous snores would mask any sound he might make, short of banging on a pan and shouting at them.

Slocum stopped by Spence's tent, thinking to find the foreman in his cot. The tent was empty. He wondered if Spence still hunted for him or if the foreman had hightailed it. A quick search failed to unearth the small map he had found before. Either it had blown away or Spence had retrieved it. Rather than waste more time, Slocum left Spence's tent and stepped out into the middle of the camp wondering what the hell he was going to do now.

The camp seemed alien to Slocum now, a bit of his past that he had already left far behind. He turned to head up the mountain toward the railroad tracks, thinking to lie low and catch the train on its way back tomorrow from Willits, but a flare of light in Faith's cabin halted him. Slocum knew he ought to ignore it, but he couldn't.

On cat's feet, he made his way to the cabin. Faith had drawn her curtains, but he saw a faint shadow moving about inside. He chewed on his lower lip, wondering what he ought to do. He went around to the door and rapped twice.

"Who's there?" Faith said quickly.

"Slocum," he answered, not wanting to call out his name too loudly. He didn't think Spence was in camp, but he didn't want to take any chances. Moreover, being seen at this time of night going into Faith's cabin would ruin her reputation and possibly put her life in jeopardy. Slocum knew how desperate Spence could get.

The man might be sweet on Faith Gaynor, but if it came down to murdering her or waltzing away from whatever scheme Spence and Elliot were involved in, Slocum knew which it would be.

The door opened and soft yellow light drifted out. Faith clutched a thin shawl about her. The light managed to work through the flimsy nightgown she wore, seductively outlining her trim body.

"John! I never thought I'd see you again, the way Spence ran you off."

"I'm like a bad penny," Slocum said, grinning. "I keep coming back."

"When I least expect it," she said. Faith looked around, then stepped back and silently urged him to enter her cabin. Slocum slipped inside and turned to her.

"You're a sight for sore eyes," he said.

"You look as if you've been chasing through the forest all night," Faith said, eyeing him from head to toe. Then she smiled and threw her arms around his neck. "And I'm glad to see you again." The redhead clung tightly to him. It didn't take Slocum but a second to realize she needed comforting, that something was terribly wrong.

He asked. She turned her lovely pale face up to his and sniffed, holding back tears.

"Everything's going wrong for us. Father so desperately needs this job and . . . and the company is losing too much money to go on much longer."

"What's his boss say?"

"Mr. Johnson would fire him in a flash if he knew. Father doesn't dare go to him for more money. Mr. Johnson said he'd gotten his last bank loan. I'm not sure if he can't get any more or doesn't want to. But the disgrace!"

Slocum understood that a proud man like Ed Gaynor would hesitate letting anyone know of his problems. What struck Slocum as strange was how a logging operation feeding one of the biggest building booms the West had ever seen could be losing money.

"What's happening?" Slocum asked. "Where's the money going?"

"We can't get skilled lumberjacks. The logging is going much slower than we need to pay the bills."

"Spence isn't working the men enough to make their time pay off for the company," Slocum said, altering her words a little.

"Perhaps so. But we *are* shorthanded. And no one will

work for us. The Indian raids are frightening men who would otherwise be eager to come here. There is some sort of trouble with that awful government agent too."

"Elliot," Slocum said. He didn't bother her with what he knew of Spence and Elliot being in cahoots. "He's trying to get Daniel to sign papers saying the Fort Bragg Lumber Company is intruding on a Pomo burial plot."

"It's like a house of cards and it is all tumbling down. What are we going to do, John?" She turned those bright blue eyes to him, and he knew he couldn't let Spence get away with his con game. Even if he hadn't wanted revenge for the foreman trying to kill him, Slocum wasn't going to walk away now.

"I've got a score to settle with a lot of men," he said grimly. "At least one I don't even have a name for." The back of his head throbbed as he remembered being slugged from behind. "That means someone besides Spence in your crew is likely working against you."

"Why?"

The map came vividly to mind. But what did it mean?

"I'm going to find out."

Faith clung tightly to him again. "I feel so much better hearing that, John. I was worried that you had just ridden off after Spence fired you. I couldn't get Father to listen to reason. He thinks it is all his fault the way the company is failing."

"He's wrong. There's more going on than any of us understand. Yet," Slocum added.

Faith turned her face back to his. This time her tear-bright eyes showed something more. She half-closed her eyelids and parted her ruby lips. Slocum kissed her. For a moment time hung as if by a thread, motionless and fragile. Then passion seized both of them.

The kiss deepened until Slocum's heart was like a trip-hammer in his chest. Faith pressed even harder against him. He felt her breasts flatten, then the nipples turn to hard little points threatening to poke holes in him. He stripped off his shirt. The gunbelt and Colt Navy followed. As he worked to remove his clothes, Faith shrugged out of the shawl. The nightgown followed quickly.

Gloriously naked, the redhead stood in the middle of the cabin watching him. Slocum hesitated. He wanted to strip off the rest of his clothes, but the sight of her nakedness was a long drink of cool water on a hot summer day.

"You're beautiful," he said.

"So are you, but you are terribly overdressed," Faith said impishly. She helped him get out of his boots and jeans. "But at least you've still got something on," she said, kneeling in front of him. Her trembling fingers reached out and cupped his balls. Hesitantly, she kissed the tip of his manhood.

A tremor passed through Slocum's body as if he had been hit by a war club. The tremor turned to sheer delight when her lips opened and she took him into her mouth. Her eager tongue worked all over the crown, then slipped back and forth on the underside until he was shifting his weight from one foot to the other, wanting more than her mouth around his meaty shaft.

He lifted her, kissed her lips, her throat, and lower. He licked and kissed and suckled at her breasts. He felt her heart running as fast as his when he shoved his tongue into the hard red nubbin capping one breast. Then he reached around her body and cupped her buttocks, pulling her powerfully into his body.

"Oh, oh!" she gasped. The passionate redhead lifted one slender leg and curled it around his waist. This pressed her crotch into his. When she rose onto her toes, then settled back down, he slid easily into her hot, tight fastness.

Slocum's arms circled her sleek nakedness and held her tight. His hands lifted the twin mounds of her rump before he began kneading them like mounds of dough. Every time he squeezed down, a tiny sound of sheer joy escaped from Faith's lips.

But the real excitement came lower. Slocum felt himself surrounded by her clinging warmth. Every time Faith gasped, her inner muscles clamped down firmly on him. He felt as if he had slipped into a tight velvet glove. The moisture flowing from her interior convinced him she was alive, she was real, she was ready for what he had to do.

The fires of carnal desire leaped in his loins. He began thrusting, short, quick strokes to stir her passion quickly. Faith was soon panting and gasping and thrashing about in his grip.

"Don't toy with me, John. Do it. Do it! Hard!"

He started making longer thrusts into her inner reaches. The woman's steamy core tensed and relaxed around him, massaging his column until he fought to keep from erupting like a geyser. She ground her crotch down into his when he buried himself all the way, then tensed and tried to hold him inside as he retreated.

He worked faster. The friction of movement ignited their desires and fanned them into a raging forest fire that knew no bounds. Slocum swung her around and pinned Faith against a cabin wall to get more leverage. She lifted the leg that had supported her and wrapped both legs tightly around his waist.

The small, short strokes turned long, hard, fast. Together they gasped out their mutual ecstasy. Faith clung to him as he drove his fleshy spike into her needy interior.

"More, John, yes, more, oh, oh!"

This time her climax carried Slocum along with it. Panting and sweaty, he stepped back. Faith's feet dropped back to the floor but she was too weak to stand. He caught her up and carried her to her bed, then lay beside her.

For a long time, neither said a word. Their hands played over one another's body and then it was time to start again. All the way till morning.

15

Slocum stared past the thin, frilly curtain in the window out into the camp—or what he could see of it. The fog had drifted in while he and Faith slept, cutting off vision almost entirely. Slocum knew he would be both blind and almost deaf if he stepped outside. The curious nature of the fog muffled sound as well as sight. In a way, it was nothing more than a gray snowstorm. He had seen the same dampening of senses in more than one blizzard. The only difference lay in the warmth and the lack of wind blowing the fog around.

Staring into the shifting gray fingers of fog and trying to make sense out of them only caused Slocum's thoughts to spin out of control. He felt so close to the answers, yet they always eluded him if he got too close. The answers were like the eternally drifting fog. Grab a handful and end up with . . . nothing.

"John?" said Faith's sleepy voice.

"I'm looking out for Spence," he said.

"He would never dare barge in on me," she said. "I told him off good when he fired you. He even avoids me when we happen to pass in camp."

Slocum knew that was not good. It put Faith in the line of fire more than she knew. All that had kept her

safe from Spence and Elliot's scheming had been the
foreman's letch for her. If pressed, Spence would give
in to his lust and forget about civilized courting. After
all, he intended to steal control of the company away
from Faith's father.

Slocum turned and asked, "Has anyone made an offer
for the lumber company?"

Faith propped herself up on one elbow. The sheet fell
slightly from her swanlike throat and exposed the barest
hint of a naked breast.

"I advised Father to consider presenting two offers we
received to Mr. Johnson, but he decided not to. The offers weren't good enough."

"Who made the offers?" Slocum thought Elliot might
be behind them.

"Competitors. Both have offered Mr. Johnson a considerable amount for our patch of forest before. The offers now are much less. They know we are in trouble."

"Vultures circling," Slocum said. He wondered if
those competitors were backed by Elliot or were legitimate businesses. Somehow, Slocum thought Elliot and
Spence were acting on their own. He didn't believe,
however, that they wanted to horn in on the lumbering
business. If anything, the claim by the Pomo that the
lumbering went on over a sacred burial ground would
prevent any other company from coming in to this section of redwood forest.

"I suppose," Faith said glumly. "Something must be
done soon, though. When Mr. Johnson finds out how
poorly Father has managed the company in his absence,
he will surely fire him."

"Your pa's up against more than he realizes," Slocum
said. He remembered how adamant Ed Gaynor had been
about not going against Spence. Gaynor shuffled papers
and arranged loans. He had no idea what it meant to go

out in the forest and actually saw down one of the red-wood giants. When the supply of wood declined, his solution would be to shuffle more papers rather than replace Spence.

"What will it take to convince the marshal something's wrong out here?" Slocum asked, more to himself than to Faith. He stared back into the swirling fog and made horrible monsters out of the vapor.

"Marshal Finnegan is a horrible man," Faith declared. She got out of bed. Slocum watched as she slowly dressed. The woman seemed oblivious to his gaze and soon had on her clothing, decent once more and ready to set to work. Slocum realized he had to follow her example. He began dressing and getting ready for what needed doing.

"He hates C. R. bad enough to throw in with Elliot and Spence?" asked Slocum.

"I don't know. He collects money from many businesses in Fort Bragg to look the other way when they do illegal things," she said.

"Such as?"

Faith shrugged. "Many companies keep slaves, but they're only Chinese. I know that's not supposed to be done, but, Finnegan takes money to allow it. He finds picayune reasons to put men out of business if they don't pay."

"But Johnson avoided that and never paid. How'd he do that?"

"Mr. Johnson has political ties," she said.

"They won't help him out if it looks like he's going under," Slocum said, knowing the way political friends operated. There would no longer be anything in the friendship for them if Johnson lost his control over the company—or the Indian claim sounded as if it had an iota of truth to it.

Slocum had to find something patently illegal, prove it, and then dare Finnegan to arrest Spence and Elliot and the unknown ambusher in the forest. If the lawman didn't, Slocum had to take care of them himself. That probably meant a new wanted poster would be put out for him.

So be it.

"I want to stir the pot a mite," Slocum said, coming to his decision. "I want you to go to your pa and have him tell Spence and anyone else who'll listen that everything's fine, that he got a loan from a distant relative to keep the company going. Have him spend like there's no tomorrow. Give bonuses, buy equipment he might have been putting off, let the money flow."

"We hardly have enough to meet next month's payroll," Faith said. "What if your plan, whatever it is, doesn't work?"

"Then the company goes under a month sooner," Slocum pointed out. "If it does work, I'll have the goods on the men trying to destroy the Fort Bragg Lumber Company. After that, it might be a struggle for a while, but the thorn will be out of your hide and healing can begin."

"I don't know, John."

"Do it. We have to flush out Spence, force him to make a mistake. If it looks like the company'll prosper after all he's done to ruin it, he might panic. I don't see him as a patient man." For all that, Slocum didn't see Elliot as being overly endowed with forbearance either. They were greedy men and wanted to get their hands on whatever it was that was blocked now by the lumber company's operation.

"All right, but I wish I knew what this would accomplish," Faith said.

Slocum didn't know either.

He kissed her and said, "I need to find Daniel. The last I saw him he was in Fort Bragg."

"Chief Daniel?" Faith laughed. "He's got a tent pitched at the edge of camp, on the side opposite the Celestials. They fight like dogs and cats now that Daniel tells them he is a chief."

"Find your pa and get him to loosen the purse strings. I'll talk to Daniel about the government agent's doings."

Slocum slipped into the clammy fog, got his bearings, and walked through the thick mist, lost in a world of his own. He almost fell over Daniel's tent due to the limited visibility caused by the fog.

"Chief, you in there?" called Slocum.

"I am here," Daniel replied. The Pomo chief sat cross-legged in the center of his tent. Slocum went inside, sat beside him, and waited for the Indian to speak.

"You hunt Spence," Daniel finally said. "He is in camp."

"I'm using something other than a gun to hunt that varmint," Slocum said. "I want to know everything about what Elliot wanted you to sign."

"The burial ground?" asked Daniel. "There is none, but he offered me—and my tribe—much to claim there was one."

"What are you going to do?"

"I am now paid by another lumber company," Daniel said. "I do not need to lie."

"What?" This startled Slocum. "You have a job with a competing lumber company?"

Chief Daniel nodded once.

"Which one?"

"California Redwood Corporation." Daniel pronounced each word carefully, as if these were difficult words to remember. "They need me as a director. I tell them of Pomo tradition, nothing more."

Slocum digested this. Elliot had given up trying to get Daniel to declare Gaynor was allowing the company to operate in an old burial ground, but the Pomo saw nothing strange about the new company offering him employment to do essentially nothing.

"Why are you camped here?" Slocum asked. "Why not camp with this California Redwood Company?"

"Corporation," corrected Daniel. "My duty is to sit and observe, then tell the other directors of techniques in cutting."

This was as outrageous as anything Slocum had ever heard. He bid the chief good-bye and slipped into the forest before the sun burned off the fog for the day. He stayed close, and heard Ed Gaynor make an impassioned speech about how the company had been rescued by a bequest from a relative back East who had died and left him a great deal of money. A cheer went up from the assembled lumberjacks, but Slocum could not see Spence's face nor hear him cheering with the others.

Slocum spent the rest of the day trying not to be seen as he followed Spence around. The foreman kept his crew working, at least until Rufus broke a crosscut saw. This brought work to a halt, and Spence told the men to take the rest of the afternoon off.

"Come on, men, let's find us some of that corn likker we hid the other day and celebrate," called Rufus. "We got the whole danged day off, so let's spend it right!"

The men scattered, forcing Slocum to circle the work area when Spence slipped away. Rufus kept the men stirred up with promises of liquor, but it was Spence that Slocum wanted. And he lost him. By the time he skirted the vicinity of the huge sequoia the lumberjacks had worked to fell, the foreman had vanished into the thicket.

Slocum tried tracking, and eventually gave up. Spence

had hurried somewhere, undoubtedly carrying the news that Gaynor was able to keep the company going. Slocum smiled thinly. His plan was working. Now to see what game he flushed out beating the bush.

The gunshots caught Slocum's attention. He had spent the afternoon sleeping in the woods not a hundred yards from the main camp. He sat up, and it took him a few seconds to locate the source of the commotion.

He grabbed his six-shooter and dashed toward the camp, not sure what he would find. Slocum had thought Spence would wait until dark to make his move, whatever it might be. Now Slocum was worried that the foreman had rushed into action.

He skidded to a halt and pressed close to a spruce tree, peering around it. In the camp stood several of the lumberjacks. One held a rifle in his hands, as if he had little idea what to do with it. He had been the one doing the shooting, but Slocum wondered if it hadn't been a drunken mistake.

Then he saw it wasn't. Ed Gaynor came out of the office. He was drawn and his hands shook far more than they had before. With a nervous gesture, Gaynor wiped his lips before speaking.

"A hundred dollars. A thousand to the man who gets her back!" Gaynor said. "But be careful. I don't want my daughter hurt." Gaynor stared at the logger holding the rifle so clumsily.

Slocum needed to know what was going on. He saw no reason to stay in hiding. He shoved his way through the loggers and grabbed Gaynor's arm spinning the man around.

"What's happened?" he demanded. Gaynor stared at him as if he were nothing more than fog. The man's eyes fixed *through* him rather than on him. Slocum had

seen men in battle so shocked by the near explosion of
shells that they looked the same.

Or men who had been pushed too far and were on the
verge of giving up on life. That was how Ed Gaynor
appeared.   ·

"Tell me."

"You caused this," Gaynor said. "You put her up to
that wild scheme."

"Where's Faith?"

"Gone. They kidnapped her," Gaynor said, all emotion flushed out of his words. He had the look of the
dead in eye and voice.

Slocum shoved Gaynor back into the office. Standing
in front of the lumberjacks solved nothing when he
thought he knew who was responsible for the crime. A
quick roll call would show Spence missing.

"How do you know?" Slocum asked, knowing Gaynor
had some proof or he wouldn't have reacted so badly.

"I . . . I found this when I came in." Gaynor pushed a
strip ripped from Faith's blue dress across the small
desk. Slocum recognized it as the dress the woman had
put on when he was with her. Tied to the end of the
ribbon of cloth was a note. Slocum unfolded and read
it.

We have her. Do as we tell you—or else.

"What are they asking for her return?" Slocum asked.

"What? The ransom? Why, I don't know. The note
says they took Faith, but they didn't say what they
wanted." Gaynor was too confused to be any help.

"This means they'll contact you later," Slocum said,
his mind racing. The federal marshal might be dragged
out of Fort Bragg to investigate but from all Faith had
said about Marshal Finnegan, Slocum wanted to handle

this himself. Besides, he had caused it. He should have realized that rats backed into a corner would snap out.

"If anything happens to her . . ." Gaynor sat on the desk and cried, face buried in his hands.

Slocum ran his fingers over the smooth butt of his six-shooter, thinking how he might get the information he wanted from Spence. But finding him would be hard. Find the foreman, find Faith Gaynor.

A hesitant knock sounded at the door. Slocum yanked it open to find Chief Daniel standing on the steps.

"We got problems, Chief," Slocum said. "We can talk later."

"I have a strange note for you. For Mr. Gaynor," the Pomo chief said. He held it out in such a way that Slocum realized Daniel didn't know how to read.

"Where'd you get this?"

"Spence told me to give it to you, to Mr. Gaynor." The Pomo seemed as confused as Gaynor by what was going on. Slocum realized Spence had used Daniel as a cat's-paw. If they brought in the law, Daniel was the only one making any demands. And who would arrest Daniel thinking he had anything to do with the kidnapping? Spence was playing this cagy, and that worried Slocum. He had wanted to force the man's hand, to rush him and cause him to blunder. Instead, Spence had been shrewder than Slocum had given him credit for.

Slocum grabbed the scrap of paper from the Indian's hand and unfolded it. He read it through twice but did not understand. And then he pieced it all together.

"What's it say? How much do they want? I'll give them anything," Gaynor said.

"You're supposed to sign over control of the company to the California Redwood Corporation." Slocum stared at Daniel. "To do that, you put Daniel in control."

"But I don't own the company. C. R. does!"

"There's no threat in the message," Slocum said, "but I think we both know what is meant. If you don't give control of the company to Chief Daniel, they'll kill Faith."

16

"I only did what was asked," Daniel said, looking aggrieved. "I like Miss Gaynor. She is always good to me."

"Nobody's blaming you," Slocum said, thinking hard about what to do next. "These are desperate men and they're willing to use anyone for their own purposes." He blamed himself more for not posting a dependable guard to watch over Faith. Hindsight told him she was the weak link in his scheme, the axle around which the ill-conceived trap spun. Take her out and everything fell apart. Ed Gaynor would do anything to get his daughter back. And Slocum was sure Spence thought Slocum would do likewise.

"We find her," Daniel said. "I know the forest. You and I, Slocum, we can find her."

"We're going to try," Slocum said, determination growing. He didn't much care now if he found the third partner in Spence and Elliot's land-grabbing scheme. He would kill both men when they came into his gun sights and never hesitate. It was one thing to fight a man face-to-face, or even gun him down from ambush. It was nothing less than cowardly to kidnap a woman.

"Don't like Elliot," Daniel said. "He got me drunk. The marshal put me in jail. It stinks. Everyone pisses in corner."

161

Slocum had to smile. "You wouldn't like having the lumber company signed over to you either, unless I miss my guess. This is a one-way ticket to prison. They'd have you convicted of a dozen different crimes and shipped off before you knew what happened."

Daniel nodded wisely, but Slocum doubted he had any idea what was at stake.

"You can't do anything to risk my daughter's life," Gaynor protested. "They'll kill her!"

"You're not the owner of the company," Slocum said. "I can't imagine Johnson going along with this either. They want you to do nothing while they continue their plan to get control of the land." Slocum's mind raced. He had already bluffed, and they had called him. It was time to deal a new hand and stop bluffing. "Don't stop the lumbering. Keep the trees going to the sawmill, no matter what the cost. That's the way to fight them."

"But, Slocum, they have Faith!"

Slocum didn't want to worry the man further, but he suspected Spence and Elliot would kill her no matter what her father did. The instant she no longer served their purpose, she would die. They had to kill her. Otherwise, even Marshal Finnegan would have to arrest them if a living, breathing, angry woman accused Elliot and Spence of kidnapping.

About that time, her connection with a man like C. R. Johnson would come into play too. Johnson would never allow his superintendent's daughter to be ignored, especially if it meant he could embarrass the marshal.

Politics took too much figuring. Slocum wanted to cut right to the heart of the matter. Find Faith. Kill her kidnappers. Cut *their* hearts out.

"They won't have her long. I'll see to that. But you need someone to oversee your crew. Why don't you get Rufus to act as foreman?" Slocum remembered how Rufus had helped him—and that Rufus owed him for saving his life.

"All right. I'll ask," Gaynor said. "How will I know when you've succeeded and I can stop the charade of being afloat with money?"

"When Faith is back," Slocum said. He jerked his head in the direction of the forest. Daniel picked up a few items piled at his feet and they started off together, leaving behind the lumber camp and the troubles brewing there.

"Where do we start?" asked Daniel, fumbling with the debris he had collected.

"Put down that junk," Slocum said, seeing how hard it was for a scavenger like Daniel to leave behind even a small treasure. "You're the one who knows the forest. Where would be a good place to hide a captive?"

"Oh, anywhere," the small Indian said, waving his arm to indicate the thick redwood forest. "There is so much out there in emptiness." He gestured in even more dramatic circles, taking in the entire world. "I like these woods. They are comfortable for me and my people."

Slocum checked the largest of the footpaths around the camp and found one kicked up more than the others. He had no idea if this was the direction Spence had dragged Faith, but he hoped so. A hundred yards along the path he got his reward.

Daniel saw the scrap of cloth from Faith's blue dress on the thorn bush the same time Slocum did. They exchanged knowing looks, then set to tracking in earnest now that they were on the right path. Slocum watched as Daniel weaved back and forth across the trail. He had not counted much on the short Pomo for help, but saw the man knew his business.

"That way," Daniel said, pointing away from the trail and the obvious footprints left by Spence.

Slocum knelt and examined the prints, then nodded. Spence had been carrying Faith, probably draped over his shoulder like a sack of flour. The depth of his boots showed his load was gone now, although he continued along the trail. Somewhere nearby he had gotten rid of Faith's weight. Whether he thought to lead them astray or chased other interests while his partner took care of Faith, Slocum could not tell. Their first chore was saving the kidnapped redhead.

He didn't like letting Spence go on his way, but knew Daniel was right. Less than ten feet into the undergrowth they saw broken twigs and trampled weeds. No distinct footprint recorded itself on the soft, squishy vegetation, but the trail was fresh. They headed downhill toward Pudding Creek, Slocum pushing the pace in his eagerness to rescue Faith. But Daniel laid a hand on his shoulder, stopping him.

The Pomo pointed into the gigantic trees. Slocum looked up. For a moment, he did not understand. Then he realized the birds had stopped singing. There was hardly a buzz of insects in the air. He frowned and shrugged, trying to ask Daniel silently what it meant.

The Indian pointed downhill, then tapped his own chest and Slocum's and indicated they should take a course parallel to the river below. Slocum started to protest, then heard movement in the forest below them. Lots of it. A single man blundering through the woods might make that much, but he doubted it.

Slocum followed Daniel, amazed anew at how silently the man moved when he put his mind to it. When the Pomo suddenly dived and fell to the ground, Slocum followed his lead. From their right came more sounds of incautious movement. Then Slocum saw what Daniel had already detected.

Three Pomo warriors blundered along. Considering

how they staggered, they had imbibed more than a little too much firewater. Slocum watched in silence, recognizing them as the ones responsible for shooting up the railroad and making life hell around the Fort Bragg Lumber camp. The Pomo he had captured had admitted they were paid by Elliot.

Slocum used sign language to show he wanted to follow the trio of Indians. If Elliot hired them, they might be on their way to his camp—and Faith Gaynor.

Daniel nodded curtly, then rose, his eyes on the retreating Indians. He bent over and began his slow creeping after them. Slocum saw how hard it was not to overtake the three Pomo. They spent more time staggering from side to side than they did going forward. Chafe as he might at waiting for the trio to pass, Slocum knew stealth was their best weapon right now. He wanted to beat Faith's location out of the three Indians, but that wouldn't be as fast as this slow stalking.

The three angled down toward the river, reaffirming Slocum's belief that Elliot had a camp nearby. He wished he had a better grasp of his surroundings to see if the site didn't match one of the Xs on the map he had found in Spence's bedroll. Something told Slocum they were near what ought to be a marked spot.

Daniel pulled him down. Slocum had been thinking and not paying attention. The three Indians had been joined by two others, who were not drunk.

"They saw me," Slocum said, realizing he had made a mistake. He reached for his pistol, but Daniel put his hand on his wrist and shook his head. The Pomo chief rose and revealed himself clearly to the five. Before Slocum could caution him, Daniel rattled off a long speech in a tone that seemed downright arrogant.

Slocum wiggled about and peered through some wildflowers at the five Indians Daniel had called to. They fingered their weapons but did not make a hostile move. Coming closer, they stared at him as if he had grown two heads.

"I am Chief Daniel, of the Pomo. Who are you to be running about on tribal land?" Daniel said loudly so Slocum could understand what was going on.

"Chief? We got no chief," said one of the drunker Indians. A backhanded slap sent him staggering. One of the sober braves had obviously chosen to exert his power and prestige.

"How is it an eater of white man's garbage calls himself chief?" asked the sober one. His belligerent tone put Slocum on edge. A fight was brewing.

"I have been made chief, and I *am* chief. Do you dispute my right?" Daniel called, thrusting out his thin chest and putting his balled hands on his hips. He looked like a real chief putting a subordinate in his place.

"You would fight me?" demanded the other, astounded at such effrontery. He looked at the braves with him to be sure he had not misunderstood Daniel's challenge. The other four were as amazed.

"Yes, but only after you sober up," Daniel said.

"I'm not drunk. They are!" cried the Indian, pointing to his comrades.

"You take orders from the government man. You are drunk with his money, if not with his firewater. You are *his* to do with as he pleases!"

"We take money and tobacco from Elliot," the Indian agreed. "We are not his slaves. We do this because we choose!"

"Then you are garbage eaters too," said Daniel. "You shoot at unarmed men. You yell at the iron horse."

"We stop them from cutting trees," said the other sober Pomo.

"This is our land, true," Daniel said. "What do you

gain working for Elliot? Do the white men go away?"

"He wants them off our land. When they leave, we will again roam these woods as our birthright."

"Others have gone to Mt. Shasta," Daniel said. "Join them. Return when I have dealt with the government man, who does bad things. He takes squaws not his."

"That is honorable way of gaining a wife," said one Indian. "We saw the red-haired woman in his camp." He turned and pointed downhill, in the direction Slocum had hoped Elliot and Faith had gone. It took all his resolve not to jump to his feet and go dashing down after the woman.

"He would kill the white squaw," Daniel said. "He does not want her for his own."

This set the five Indians to talking among themselves. Slocum held his breath, wondering whether if he cut down two or three, Daniel could kill the rest. He doubted it. He had to let the self-styled chief finish, without alerting Elliot or Spence so they could harm Faith.

"We know he has the woman, but we thought she was plunder," one Indian said.

"He stole her away in the dead of night," Daniel said, embellishing the story a mite. "He is a coward, as you are if you continue to take his money and smoke his tobacco."

It amazed Slocum how they accepted Daniel on his own terms. What struck him as even more startling was the mantle of authority Daniel had adopted naturally once he had been told to pretend he was a chief.

"You call us cowards?"

Daniel shrugged, then said, "Yes."

"We will fight!" challenged one of the drunken Indians.

"No, you will follow the spirit trail to Mt. Shasta and not return until your soul is cleansed," Daniel said imperiously. "This is our way. You are not slaves."

"Not Elliot's slave!" protested one. "We *take* from the white man."

"Then go," Daniel said. "When you return purified and whole, then we will fight."

Slocum couldn't believe the five warriors actually argued again about obeying Daniel. When they reluctantly nodded and headed off into the forest, Slocum was astonished.

"Are they really leaving?" he asked.

"They have shot at enough white men for the time," Daniel said, settling down on his heels. "They will renew their spirits, then return."

"To kill you?"

Daniel smiled crookedly. "If they can find me. If I have not gathered enough followers. If I have not found heart to fight them for the right to be chief of my tribe."

"You surely do take that seriously," Slocum said, watching as the five Indians vanished. A major part of Spence and Elliot's fighting force was eliminated, if the Indians were truly leaving the coast for the distant inland mountain.

"Never been chief before. Have to take it seriously," Daniel said solemnly.

Slocum didn't know if he was joking. It hardly mattered because they were much closer to finding Faith. Slocum knew the five weren't far from Elliot's camp and had pointed in the right direction.

It was getting close to rescue—and revenge—time. Slocum felt it deep in his gut.

17

"If the creek meanders along like this," Slocum said, drawing a wiggly line in the dirt of the forest floor, "where would we look for *this* spot?" He tried to place the X the best he could from memory on his crude map.

"Creek not moving along like that. Straight here, not wiggling," Daniel said.

"Those Pomo you chased off," he said, still flabbergasted at the way Daniel had taken control of the dangerous situation so naturally, "must have been heading for this spot. That's where Elliot is." Slocum was sure of it.

"Pudding Creek?" Daniel pointed to Slocum's map.

"Sure, why not?"

"Noyo River a mile over there," Daniel said, stabbing his finger to the south. "Looks more like this." He indicated the crude map Slocum had made, with its Xs.

"Is that part of the river still on the lumber company property?" Slocum asked. Daniel nodded once. "So we might be looking in the wrong place for Faith?"

Again Daniel nodded once.

Slocum stood and set off for the distant Noyo River. Time was a-wasting. With a long, ground-devouring stride, Slocum made his way down the side of the hill.

Twenty minutes later, at the bottom near the quick-running Pudding Creek, Slocum stopped and listened hard. He expected to hear the sawing as Rufus worked the crew to bring down another of the redwood giants. He didn't hear it.

"There, ahead, up and over hill," Daniel said, pointing to the far side of the creek. They still had a far amount of hiking to do, but Slocum was up for it. It was Slocum's turn to nod assent. The would-be Pomo chief crossed the swift, deep creek, finding fallen logs and rocks to use as stepping-stones, then huffed and puffed as he hiked up the far side of the canyon, meandering in and out through the trees. Slocum kept up easily, his mind already casting ahead to how he might launch a one-man attack on Elliot.

It depended on Elliot and how many men were gathered around to hold Faith captive.

"Are there spots around here where your tribe cremated their dead?" Slocum asked. He still sought any burial ground or something passing for it.

"Funerals are wherever it is private," Daniel said. "Dead pass from this life to next. Where they leave matters less than how well they are sent away."

Slocum grabbed the Indian and pulled him down when he spotted a thin wisp of smoke curling up from a cabin chimney just over the top of the ridge. He put his finger to his lips, urging Daniel to silence. Then he indicated the Pomo was to stay put while he scouted. Slocum had no idea how good Daniel might be at spying. He had lived in the forest; he might know a great deal. After all, the man seemed to have an incredible amount of heart, and showed bravery when Slocum least expected it. But this was a personal matter, and Slocum didn't want anyone, Daniel or the law or anyone else, butting in.

Moving slowly, he flitted from bush to bush, and finally found cover not fifteen feet from the cabin's front door. A patch had been cleared, leaving only ankle-high weeds, making an approach any closer dangerous. Slocum settled down, watched the way the white smoke curled upward, and decided that someone was feeding the fire. More smoke came out now than had a few minutes ago.

That meant the occupants of the cabin might be fixing some grub. Slocum could use some since his belly protested that his throat must have been cut, shutting off a steady flow of food. But he forgot that slight discomfort when he saw how he could get closer. Circling, Slocum went to the side of the cabin. He bent low and peered through a spot between logs where the mud had dried and fallen out.

Slocum pressed his eye to the peephole. He was disappointed with the limited view he got. He recoiled when a boot passed within inches of his eye. He feared he might have been seen, but the foot moved on, then went to the middle of the cabin. Prying loose more of the caked mud, Slocum got a better view.

Elliot stood in the center of the cabin, holding a plate filled with food that sent up tiny curls of steam. The man forked the food into his mouth. His attention seemed fixed on something across the cabin. Slocum worried out more mud, this time a few logs higher, and peeked inside. He caught his breath when he saw Faith Gaynor, securely tied to a straight-backed chair pushed up to a table.

"You want food, don't you?" taunted Elliot. "You won't get it, not until that worthless papa of yours gives in."

"I hope he calls your bluff!" she said gamely.

"Bluff? Who's bluffing? We'll kill you if he doesn't

do everything we want," Elliot said. The government man forked in a few more mouthfuls of food, then leered at her. "We'll kill you after we've gotten to know you a bit better."

"You animal!"

"Me? I'm real civilized. Got a college education, even if none of them yahoos back in Fort Bragg appreciates the fact. No, it's the Indians that are the real animals. They'll especially enjoy you—over and over until they get all tuckered out. They don't get many white women to do with as they like. A red-haired white woman will be a special treat for them, I understand. Watching them have their fun is going to be a whole load of fun for me too!" Elliot laughed harshly and finished shoveling his food into his mouth.

"My father'll kill you!"

"Gaynor's a lily-livered coward," Elliot said. "He doesn't have the spine to stand up to his own crew. How's he ever going to find out what happened to you, unless I tell him? Think I'd like to see him suffer when I do tell him how much they enjoyed your favors. I never liked that sanctimonious son of a bitch much. He always treated me poorly, like some kind of vermin."

Slocum's hand touched his gun, but he did not draw. The man didn't head for his captive. Instead, he went back to the fireplace and ladled out more food onto his tin plate. Elliot seemed intent on stuffing himself— whether to torment a starving Faith or simply because he was hungry, Slocum didn't care. Elliot wasn't going to do anything to her for a while. He was too busy baiting her.

Slocum backtracked and slipped into the dense forest, letting it swallow him whole. He wondered if Daniel would do something stupid, then pushed it from his mind. The Indian was likely to stay where he was for a bit longer. This gave Slocum the chance to look around. If this was one of the two Xs marked on Spence's map, something important had to be nearby. The other X had been a short distance upriver. The Noyo River, Slocum told himself.

He drifted like a shadow through the forest, and then hastened down to the river, where he found the reason for Spence and Elliot's behavior. A crude, poorly constructed shaker table gave way to an entire placer mine. Clear, cold water from the raging river had been diverted in hollowed-out wood logs and run into a trough high along the top of the claim, a perpetual waterfall dropping down across the table. A simple valve system increased the flow when needed. Other equipment lay scattered around the mining site, possibly built from material stolen from Gaynor's camp. The Indians might have been responsible for the thefts, but Slocum wasn't so sure. Spence could have done the thieving, even diverting the supplies before Gaynor—or Faith—got a chance to inventory the material. However it worked, a considerable amount of expensive equipment had been assembled for use in the clandestine placer mine.

Someone had worked the riverside mine for quite a spell, maybe months. Slocum poked about the debris at the base of the placer and found quartz bits. In the piles of dirt waiting to be shoveled into the equipment were shining specks of a mineral he recognized instantly. This inspired him to see how rich this might prove.

Slocum cupped his hands, scooped the dirt, and dumped it into the shaker. He worked until tiny fly-specks of glittering mineral appeared at the bottom of the clear-running stream of water flowing over the wooden ridges in the table. Picking them up, Slocum placed them carefully in his palm to examine them.

"Gold," he said. This explained the lengths to which

Spence and Elliot had gone. Lumbering would cease instantly when it got out that gold had been discovered so close to the camp. As hard as mining for gold was, it would prove far more lucrative than cutting down trees, even when the market in San Francisco was limitless for the sawed wood.

Slocum carefully put the tiny flecks into his shirt pocket for safekeeping, then headed back to the cabin where Elliot held Faith. It was time to start the dance.

As he approached the cabin, Slocum began worrying about Daniel. He didn't want the Indian interfering at the wrong time or doing anything he might consider heroic that would endanger Faith. Slocum skirted the clearing in front of the cabin and headed for the spot where he had left Daniel.

Slocum frowned. His fears about the Indian messing things up might be a dead-on bull's-eye. Daniel had vanished. Slocum dropped to his knee and looked at the ground for some sign of the direction taken by the Pomo chief. Aside from a few spots where grass had been crushed down and the blades had sprung back slowly, Slocum found no sign of his companion.

He wiped his lips, beginning to worry. Daniel might have gotten bored and left for the logging camp. At least, Slocum hoped this was true. It got the Indian out of the line of fire and improved the odds of rescuing Faith unhurt.

Slocum checked his six-shooter and made sure it was fully loaded. He usually carried it with the hammer resting on an empty chamber. No longer. He wanted six shots when he tackled Elliot. Tucking it back into his cross-draw holster, Slocum set off for the cabin. He grew warier when he approached.

Daniel. Where was he? Slocum pushed the Pomo from his mind and concentrated only on the cabin, the front door, the occupants. He faded back into the forest, intending to approach for one last look to be sure Elliot still held Faith inside. As he moved through the under-growth, something caused the hair on the back of his neck to rise.

He couldn't figure what it might be. The smoke still curled from the cabin in front of him, but something was wrong.

The sound of a six-gun cocking behind him froze Slocum in his tracks and sent his heart racing.

"You caused enough trouble," came the cold words. "It's time for you to die, Slocum!"

18

Slocum turned slowly to face the Fort Bragg Lumber Company foreman. Spence had his six-shooter aimed squarely at Slocum's body.

"You been a thorn in my side since you showed up. You got Faith away from me, and you wouldn't stop pokin' your nose where it didn't belong," Spence said.

"She never even liked you," Slocum said, playing for time. If he kept Spence talking, the man might make a mistake. Since he had the drop on Slocum, how this was going to happen wasn't clear. Spence's finger tensed so much on the pistol trigger that it turned white. The slightest twitch would send a heavy lead slug into Slocum's chest.

"She did too! She was my girl. We coulda done things together. And you wouldn't quit pokin' into my scheme to get some money. It's my due, after workin' like a dog for nickels and dimes!"

"The gold mine? You trying to force Gaynor to leave the area so you and Elliot could mine to your heart's content? I was over there. I saw the placer."

"Never stop snoopin', do you?" growled Spence. "I tried to get rid of you by droppin' a whole damn redwood on your head. Still don't know how that failed.

You must have Lady Luck ridin' on your shoulder."

Slocum hadn't noticed. He would never have come north from San Francisco if he hadn't been cheated in a poker game. And he would have worked as a carpenter for a few more months, except that the scarcity of lumber had driven the construction company out of business. It seemed as if all roads had led to this moment. Slocum saw nothing lucky about any of it.

"How'd you cut through the tree trunk so fast?" he asked.

"Hell, it was mostly cut. A stick of dynamite and a blasting cap stolen from the railroad done the rest," Spence bragged. "But I'm gettin' real tired of you interferin' in my plans. Burn in hell, Slocum!" Spence raised the six-shooter and aimed it. Slocum knew this was the end.

The six-shooter exploded.

As quickly as the knowledge he was going to die hit him, so did the knowledge that Spence had not only missed, but now lay facedown on the ground, unconscious. Slocum relaxed, his hand on the ebony butt of his six-shooter. He looked behind Spence for some clue as to what had happened.

Then he went into a crouch and his six-shooter came out smoothly, cocked and aimed upward at a shadowy figure on a low branch.

"You let him sneak up," said Daniel, dropping to the ground. He dusted off his hands in satisfaction, then picked up a rock and hefted it. Smiling, the Indian dropped the rock beside Spence's prone body.

"Thanks. That's twice you saved me," Slocum said.

"The shot called out to government man in cabin, betcha," Daniel said.

Slocum cursed under his breath. The nearness of being bushwhacked by Spence had forced away his thoughts of rescuing Faith. There was no way Elliot could have missed the gunshot. Kneeling, Slocum grabbed Spence's gun and tossed it to Daniel.

"Here, you can use that, can't you?"

The Pomo hefted the six-gun and nodded once. Slocum hoped Daniel wasn't simply agreeing for the sake of agreeing. He might need some decidedly accurate fire to back him up.

"Come on," Slocum said, spinning and running toward the cabin. Outwardly, all seemed the same. The smoke curled from the chimney, and the front door was closed. But Slocum heard heavy footsteps inside the cabin and angry cursing. Elliot had been alerted, making it even more difficult to get Faith away from him.

Slocum had considered poking a hole through the wall so he could shove his six-shooter through and drill Elliot. But now Elliot would probably have his pistol to Faith's head. Any unusual sound would cause him to react. Since Slocum didn't think Elliot was all that accustomed to using a gun, that meant he would panic and start spraying lead all over the place. Faith was likely to be the first casualty.

If he had trusted Daniel's marksmanship, Slocum would have boldly walked up, hands in the air, calling out to Elliot that he wanted to palaver. Then, when the government agent showed himself, Daniel could shoot him. But Slocum doubted the Indian was that good a shot, and it did not work as well if Daniel walked up, hands in the air. Elliot was likely to put a hole in the Pomo.

Hell, for all that, Slocum wasn't sure Elliot wouldn't plug him too, if given the chance. Why talk if you could kill your enemy outright?

"Daniel," Slocum said. "Can you use that hog-leg?"

"This?" The Indian held up Spence's pistol.

"Really use it, if you have to?" demanded Slocum. "I don't mean can you pull the trigger. Can you *kill* Elliot with it?"

"Yes."

"Watch for him. If you get a clean shot and won't hit Miss Gaynor, you take it."

"What are you doing?"

"Wait and see. It won't take long to flush out that coyote," Slocum said. He holstered his pistol, made his way on the side of the cabin without a window, and began working his way to the roof. From inside he heard Elliot's angry cries. Slocum ignored them. He doubted Elliot would shoot Faith unless someone crossed him. Right now Elliot was scared and didn't have any idea what was going on.

But he would. Soon enough.

Slocum scrambled onto the roof, slipped, and almost fell on the slick surface. He got his toes buried in the rotting roof and made his way toward the chimney. The smoke rolled upward in thick billows. Slocum knocked a few stones loose and dropped them down the chimney. Then he realized this wasn't going to work. He stripped off his shirt and crammed it into the chimney. The smoke suddenly stopped floating skyward and began filling the cabin.

"You son of a bitch!" screamed Elliot. "What are you doing to me?"

Slocum went to the front, signaled Daniel to wait, then drew his six-shooter and poked it over the edge of the roof where a man might come running out of the cabin. From inside he heard Elliot continue to cuss a blue streak. Then the government agent did the worst thing possible. He tried to put out the fire by throwing water on it. The steam filled the cabin so fast it looked like a valve had broken on a locomotive. Long white plumes of steam gushed from between the logs in the walls and shot outward fully ten feet.

"I'm coming out, damn you!" cried Elliot, warning Slocum. The door opened and Elliot pushed Faith out ahead of him.

Whether by design or accident, Daniel did exactly the right thing. He discharged Spence's pistol into the air. The loud report caught Elliot's attention and turned him away from any possible threat coming down from above. He lifted his six-shooter to take a potshot at Daniel. Slocum jumped off the roof and crashed into him, knocking Faith aside as he landed with both feet on Elliot's shoulders.

Elliot fell heavily and lost his gun. Scrambling for it didn't work. Daniel fired a second shot. This one kicked up the dirt in front of Elliot's face. The man froze. This should have ended the fight, but Slocum didn't feel Elliot had been punished enough.

Getting to his feet, Slocum judged distances and took two quick, short steps. A well-placed kick to Elliot's face knocked him to the ground in a limp heap.

Slocum recovered his balance, and almost crashed into Faith as she ran crying to him.

"John, John, it was terrible. He . . . he was going to—" Tears poured down her cheeks, leaving behind muddy trails.

"I know. I heard everything he said to you." He turned her around and worked at the tight knots Elliot had used to bind her hands behind her back. Faith sagged when he released her finally.

"Oh, John, I'm so glad it's over."

"Daniel helped out a bunch," Slocum said. "He got Spence for me. And I got this one." Slocum kicked Elliot hard in the ribs. The government agent groaned but did not move. Slocum dropped to one knee and used the ropes Elliot had tied Faith with to bind the man's wrists. Slocum made sure they were cruelly tight. He didn't want Elliot getting away.

"John," Faith asked. "Why don't you have a shirt?"

Slocum laughed. "It was sacrificed for the rescue." He took her in his arms for a moment, then released her. "I want to get Elliot and Spence inside where we can watch them until Marshal Finnegan gets out here to take them to jail."

He dragged Elliot along facedown and then up and over the threshold into the cabin. The man groaned all the way. Slocum paid him no heed. Daniel stood over him, his gun pointing at the man's head, while Slocum fetched Spence. The foreman was coming around. Slocum bashed him again. It was easier dragging him too than getting him to cooperate.

Slocum lashed the two kidnapping thieves together, then coughed at the thick fog still in the cabin.

"I plugged up the chimney real good," he said.

"Can you do something about it, John?"

"I'll get my shirt," he said, smiling. "You watch them." He took the gun from Daniel and handed it to Faith, who gripped it in both hands. "And you, Chief, head on into Fort Bragg and tell the marshal to get out here with a couple deputies. We have caught him a pair of outlaws."

"Will he believe me?" asked Daniel.

"Chief, I've heard you convince a band of drunken Pomo to hightail it for Mt. Shasta. Marshal Finnegan shouldn't be any trouble at all for you."

Daniel nodded once and left without another word. Faith looked at Slocum.

"I'll explain later. Keep an eye on these two owl-hoots." Slocum went outside and clambered onto the roof, again finding it hard to walk on the decaying surface. He plucked his shirt from the chimney and shook out a few embers clinging to it. The holes burned in his shirt were minor. Worse was the way it smelled of woodsmoke.

"Could be worse," he said, putting on the shirt. He went to the edge of the roof, caught hold, and dropped over the side, landing hard on the ground. He brushed off his hands and went inside. Faith stood at the rear of the cabin, a look of horror on her face.

Slocum noticed that she didn't have the six-shooter any longer.

"All done outside," he said in a cheerful voice. He was keyed up, wondering what was wrong. From the corner of his eye he saw movement and responded fast. *Fast.*

He kicked out, caught the edge of the door, and sent it swinging back to protect him as he drew his Colt Navy. Slocum wasn't even sure who he was firing at. He went into a crouch and fanned the hammer of his six-gun as hard and fast as he could. His target was hidden in shadows. One shot. Two, three, four. Slocum kept fanning until the hammer landed on an empty cylinder.

"John!" cried Faith, shaken out of her shock.

Two bullets tore through the door partially protecting him. Then he heard a heavy six-shooter hit the floor. An instant later a heavier thud sounded.

Slocum cautiously came out of his gunfighter's crouch and kicked the other man's fallen six-shooter away. Faith snatched it up, then handed it to him.

"Take it, John. He . . . he came in right after you went up on the roof. I didn't know. I thought I could trust him."

Slocum cocked the pistol and went to the man he had drilled. Rolling him over gave Slocum quite a shock.

"Rufus," he said.

Eyelids fluttered open. The man clutched at the two bullet holes Slocum had blasted into his gut.

"Reckon it's even now, Slocum. You saved my life. Now you took it away."

"How'd you get mixed up with those owlhoots?" Slocum could hardly believe it. He had liked Rufus.

"Whod' ya think found the gold? Spence? He don't know gold from granite." Rufus coughed. "You got me good, Slocum. Damned good shooting."

"Did you slug me out in the forest and tie me to the log going downriver?" Slocum asked.

"Don't much matter now, does it?" Rufus coughed again. His eyes opened, but he wasn't looking at Slocum. Rather, he was seeing something beyond. "If it makes you feel any better, yeah, I done it. Thought it was a fine idea at the time."

Rufus heaved a sigh, twitched a mite, then died. Slocum had expected to feel better about killing the man who had tied him to the log to drown.

"Never heard a pair of galoots try so hard to out-talk each other," Marshal Finnegan said. "Elliot would tell me everything, then Spence would top him. I swear, I can clean up every last crime in the county if I let them talk long enough."

"No need for that. You got enough on them, kidnapping Miss Gaynor, inciting the Pomo to shoot up the train and Mr. Gaynor's camp, stealing anything not nailed down, and—" Slocum hesitated to go on.

"They both accused each other of trying to kill you, Slocum. Then they decided, since Rufus was dead, he was the one to blame."

"Get them out of here," Ed Gaynor said. "I don't want to see their ugly faces ever again."

"Reckon you will, Mr. Gaynor. At the trial," said Finnegan. He motioned to two deputies, who shoved Elliot and Spence from the cabin.

"I'm glad this is behind us," Gaynor said, heaving a deep sigh. "And I'm glad you saved my daughter, Slocum. Thank you."

"Daniel helped out too," Slocum said.

"Well, yes, I'm sure. Now, I have a logging company to run. I'll need a new foreman. Do you think Lou is a good choice?" Gaynor started to leave, but Daniel moved to block the man.

"Not all is done," Daniel said in his best chief's voice.

"Why, what's left?" asked Gaynor.

"Gold," Daniel said. "Gold is on Pomo tribal land."

"What! That's outrageous. The gold is on Fort Bragg Lumber Company land. I'll get a crew in to mine it and give the company extra revenue. I can—"

"No gold, no cutting trees on Pomo land," Daniel said firmly.

"You're not a chief. I appointed you chief to appease that fool Elliot. I—"

"Mr. Gaynor," Slocum said, interrupting. "Seems to me you owe Chief Daniel a great deal. Let the Pomo have the gold. The redwoods are worth far more to you and the company. If production increases, you can sell the logs for a hundred times what you could for the gold."

"I don't know," Gaynor said, stroking his stubbled chin.

"Give Daniel the gold. For his tribe," Faith urged.

"Very well. But you'll have to make your own deal with the California Western Railroad to ship it out."

Daniel nodded once, then smiled. He shook Slocum's hand, then Gaynor's, then bowed in a positively courtly fashion in Faith's direction. He followed Finnegan and his deputies to the railroad tracks to get a ride back to Fort Bragg.

"I shouldn't have given in that easily," Gaynor said. "That might be a valuable claim."

"It's rich enough," Slocum said. He had seen enough placer claims in his day to know Spence and Elliot— and Rufus—would have been well off but not wealthy from working that section of the Noyo River. "But not that rich, especially if you can negotiate a better deal in San Francisco for your lumber."

"I'm anxious to get matters squared away here. Do you think you can do that for me?" asked Gaynor.

"With some help," Slocum said, glancing at Faith. "I know I can."

19

"The Palace Hotel," Faith Gaynor exclaimed, eyes wide as she stared at the floor-to-ceiling mirrors, the exquisite hangings, the fancy translucent cut-leaded-glass chandeliers casting delicate rainbows everywhere. "I do declare. I never thought I'd stay at such a fine place. Ever." The surroundings were impeccable, the way a man— and a woman—ought to live, Slocum thought. The crystal chandeliers filled with hundreds of candles dangled down over fine Persian rugs. Everywhere he looked stood statuary, with oil paintings on the walls and other artwork scattered throughout the magnificent lobby.

A man could get to like this. Slocum looked at the equally dazzling Faith. They had stopped on the way to the hotel at a shop near Portsmouth Square and had spent an afternoon purchasing new clothing for her.

"We have business to conduct," he reminded her.

"Oh, pish," she said, dismissing him. "Business won't take too long. And that's not until tomorrow morning. We can . . . enjoy ourselves until we meet with the buyers."

It had surprised Slocum that Ed Gaynor had agreed to sending his daughter to San Francisco to negotiate the new deals with the contractors. It has surprised him even more that Gaynor had sent him along to chaperon the lovely woman. That was like putting the fox in charge of the henhouse.

Slocum counted it as a change in luck.

"We couldn't afford any of this without Chief Daniel's largesse," Faith said. She inhaled deeply, savoring the lavish surroundings as if they could be stored up and remembered.

"He's a mighty rich man now," Slocum said. "At least his tribe is." Slocum had to shake his head at the way things had turned out. Daniel now legally owned the gold mine Rufus, Spence, and Elliot had tried to steal, the intent now being that the gold would pass through to benefit the Pomo. Since there wasn't much in the way of a Pomo tribe, that meant Daniel—*Chief* Daniel—benefited most. One of his first acts had been to give the necessary travel money to Faith and Slocum.

Slocum knew Ed Gaynor had made the right decision giving Daniel the gold mine. The real treasure lay in the huge redwood forest and the lumber that would be sent down to the boom town of San Francisco. A veritable fortune could be had, one that would renew itself in a few years so it could be cut again.

Slocum had asked and the best anyone knew, it only took a handful of years for one of the huge sequoias to grow. By the time the Fort Bragg Lumber Company had finished with one section of land, they could start all over again. The gold in the stream, however, would peter out in a year or two. Maybe less.

Slocum was willing to enjoy the flood of money while it came. His luck had truly changed.

"The restaurant in the hotel is superb," Faith said. "Everyone says so. Let's eat. Then we can—"

Slocum shook his head. "I've got a little business to tend to before pleasure." He took her hand and gave it

a squeeze. "You go on. I won't be more than an hour
or two."

"Business for my father?" she asked, puzzled.

"My own business."

Slocum left her in the lobby, knowing he was a fool,
but having to do this for his own peace of mind. He
settled his Colt Navy in its holster, the leather keeper
pulled off the hammer. Quickly leaving the fancy hotel,
Slocum turned toward the Embarcadero and the dives
along the waterfront. He stopped at the base of the pier
where the Cobweb Palace disgraced the area. Drunken
sailors staggered in and out of that hellhole.

Slocum ran his fingers over the wad of greenbacks in
his shirt pocket. Daniel had been generous. So had Ed
Gaynor when it came to settling accounts.

Slocum went into the Cobweb Palace, hunting for the
sailor and his cronies who had cheated him before. Luck
rode with Slocum now. Luck and good sense. It was
time to settle scores.

He saw the sailor busily cheating a drunk at a corner
table, and went over. He kicked a chair out and sat
down, looking across the table at the bulky sailor. He
put his six-shooter on the table, then dropped his poke
beside it.

"Deal me in," Slocum said, knowing the result this
time would be different. And it was.